W9-AXF-636

WHERE EVIL SLEEPS

ALSO BY VALERIE WILSON WESLEY:

Devil's Gonna Get Him

When Death Comes Stealing

WHERE EVIL SLEEPS

Valerie Wilson Wesley

G. P. Putnam's Sons   New York

"Straight Outta Compton" (Dr. Dre/Eazy-E/Ice Cube/M.C. Ren).
Ruthless Attack Muzick (ASCAP) © 1989. Used by permission. All rights reserved.

G. P. Putnam's Sons
Publishers Since 1838
200 Madison Avenue
New York, NY 10016

Library of Congress Cataloging-in-Publication Data

Wesley, Valerie Wilson.
     Where evil sleeps / by Valerie Wilson Wesley.
          p.   cm.
     ISBN 0-399-14145-6 (acid-free paper)
     I. Title.
PS3573.E8148W49   1996
813'.54—dc20   96-19027 CIP

Printed in the United States of America

10 9 8 7 6 5 4 3 2 1

This book is printed on acid-free paper. ∞

Book design by Amanda Dewey

Again, I'd like to thank Faith H. Childs and E. Stacy Creamer for their support and encouragement. I'd also like to thank R. Robotham, K. Moses, O. Scott, E. McCampbell, M.D., C. Coker, R. Fleming, T. Harvin, and C. Virgin for their expert advice and help, and as always Richard for his love.

To my husband, Richard,
a Newark boy who is always in my corner

Evil knows where evil sleeps.

NIGERIAN PROVERB

WHERE EVIL SLEEPS

1

The man swam fast, like a witch was riding him. His skin was as smooth and dark as Jamaican rum, and he looked that strong, too. At least his arms did. Arms aren't the first thing I usually notice about a man, but I was bored and slightly drunk and there wasn't a hell of a lot else to look at or think about.

I was sitting by the pool of a joke of a hotel called the Montego Bay in the middle of Kingston, Jamaica. It was the third day of my week-long vacation. I was lonely and depressed and the city was feeling like Newark, the place where I live and work as a private investigator. I was beginning to wish I'd scraped together the money to bring my teenage son, Jamal, along, which should tell you just how bad things were.

Everything had started out fine. The ticket down had been free; you can't get any better than that. A couple months back I rescued Wyvetta Green's baby sister from the eager jaws of the New Jersey criminal justice system. Grateful Wyvetta, my good friend and owner of Jan's Beauty Biscuit, a beauty salon downstairs from my office, paid part of my fee with a ticket to Kingston. I was on my own for the hotel, so I'd made reservations at the cheapest place I could find this side of a dive.

The state of the hotel hadn't mattered much in the beginning. I spent my first night in Kingston charmed by the banana trees and bittersweet smell of the air with its trace of allspice and car exhaust. The next day I'd hit all the tourist spots touted in Frommer's guidebook — Devon House, the Bob Marley Museum, Hope Gardens — haggling with the sisters in the crafts market like a native-born daughter.

But I'd gotten up very late this morning with a crick in my neck and a bad case of the runs. I'd stayed in my room until the air conditioner and TV broke within half an hour of each other, and then made it out to the hotel restaurant, where I ordered a late breakfast from a sullen waiter with a studied British accent. The cold toast, watery eggs, and Sanka (forget Blue Mountain) told me I'd be better served by a cold rum punch by the pool, so I counted the orange slices stuck on the rim of the glass as breakfast, and settled into a lounge chair to see what I could see. What I saw was the swimmer stroking like he was headed somewhere farther than the other end of the pool. I didn't notice the woman when she sat down in the beach chair next to me and started up a conversation.

"I guess you didn't hear me. I see we been shopping at the same place for suits," she said as she peered at me over round, pink-tinted sunglasses and grinned. She was wearing the same red maillot swimsuit as me, less twenty-five pounds and about fifteen years. I tugged my cover-up farther down to hide the cellulite on my thighs and returned her smile. She was pretty the way a kid is pretty; "pert" they'd probably call her in a magazine. Her short hair was nearly the same reddish brown color as her skin, and about two dozen freckles were sprinkled like dark brown sugar across her forehead and cheeks. Her voice was little-girl high and there hadn't been a trace of attitude when she'd repeated herself. A small but expensive-looking Minolta dangled on a red string between her small breasts.

"Not that I can blame you. Hearing me, I mean. I wouldn't have heard me either," she continued, nodding toward the swimmer. She settled into the beach chair, tucking her right leg under her left, and took a sip of something in a brandy snifter that looked like curdled milk. "He's a friend of my husband's. A business associate." She stumbled over the words like they were hard to say or a bad joke. "Delaware. That's what he calls himself, even though he's really from Jersey City, the same as the rest of us. Delaware Brown. Isn't that something, how you can give yourself a name like that and everybody calls you by it?"

I nodded, fascinated by how quickly she'd engaged me in a conversation in which I'd said nothing.

"Want to meet him? Delaware Brown?"

Now that surprised me.

"No," I said quickly, more annoyed then I meant to let show. The ice had melted in my drink and it looked like flat ginger ale. I took a sip anyway, and studied the *Gleaner*, the Jamaican daily I'd picked up at the desk. She watched me for a minute.

"I'm sorry. I didn't mean to bother you. My husband says I'm a serious pain in the ass sometimes."

She said it with a sad twist of a smile that told me she was younger than I'd thought. Early twenties, maybe. Young enough to put up with some jackass telling her she was a pain in the butt. Too damn young. I folded up the newspaper and smiled. "You're fine, honey. Don't worry about it. No problem."

She giggled like the kid she was. " 'No problem.' Have you noticed everybody says that down here? 'No problem!' I'm Lilah Love." She offered me her hand. "Lilah Love. My real name is Delilah, that's what my husband calls me anyway, but I like Lilah. It's got a rhythm to it like I'm getting ready to be introduced as somebody big-time. Like a singer or nightclub star or something like that. Lilah Love. Da, da! 'And introducing Lilah Love!' " She giggled and gave a nod that was supposed to indicate a bow. I smiled politely.

"And you are?"

I hesitated for a minute. I wasn't sure why.

"Tamara Hayle."

"Hail? Like the rain that feels like snow?"

"With a *y*. H-a-y-l-e."

"That's nice. It's got a rhythm to it too. So you down here on vacation? We are." She glanced behind her as she answered her own question, and then looked around her like she was trying to think of something else to say. "Can I take your picture?"

"My picture?"

"I like the way you look." She paused for a minute, and then giggled. "I don't mean nothing fresh by it. We look like we got the same taste, and you look like you got a lot of style. I like to take pictures of people I don't know. Like maybe I was a photographer in my other life."

I studied her for a minute, not sure what to make of her.

"Okay."

She stood up and took a couple of shots, squinting and adjusting the lens like an expert. Then she sat back down, and waved to the waiter, who came over with his pad out.

"Yes ma'am, may I help you, ma'am?"

"Don't you love how polite they are? How they call everybody 'ma'am' all proper?"

"May I help you, ma'am?"

"Another Bailey's. Bailey's on ice. You want something, Tamara Hayle with a *y*?"

"No, thanks."

"You sure?"

It was so hot I could see the heat waves shimmering in the air, and I felt thirsty and slightly dehydrated as the rum punches wore off. "Okay. Some club soda, lots of ice. A twist of lime." Lilah burst out laughing, tossing her head back dramatically.

"A twist of lime! Where you from?"

"The States."

"I know that," she said, like a little girl being teased. "I know you're from the States. What part? You from the South?"

"Jersey."

"Homegirl!" she squealed, so loud the waiter glanced back. "Isn't that weird, you can go halfway around the world and meet somebody from Jersey. Jersey City? Everybody I know is from Jersey City."

"Newark."

"Newark? My daddy grew up in Newark. On Waverly Avenue. But he left to go to Jersey City before I was born. Called it bettering himself. That's funny, ain't it?" She laughed then with a bitter edge, not at all like a pert little girl. "You were born there too?"

"Yeah." I picked up the *Gleaner* again, wondering if maybe her husband had a point.

"Excuse me for a minute, I'll be right back." She patted my arm softly and left. I wondered if it was worth going back to my room to see if the air conditioner had been fixed yet, but before I could make my break she was back, holding the hand of a man who looked like a bouncer in an after-hours spot.

"Sammy Lee Love, Tamara Hayle. Tamara Hayle, Sammy Lee Love, my husband." She drawled out the word "husband" so long it sounded like a joke, but there was also a touch of something else that I couldn't identify, so I gave her the benefit of a doubt. He touched her lightly on the top of the head, as if she were a child.

Sammy Lee Love wasn't a big man—five foot seven or eight at most—but he was built squarely and solidly. He looked like he could throw a punch without feeling anything but pleasure in the throwing. He was older than Lilah, but the age in his eyes wasn't from years. He narrowed them very slightly as he looked at me, and there was a cruel glint in them.

"My wife here, Delilah, tells me you're from back home. Homegirl? That's the way she put it anyway." There was an old man's patronizing tone in his voice, but Lilah didn't seem to mind it. She just kept grinning.

"I'm from Newark."

"Good city, Newark. Been through some shit, but a good city." He looked around like he was trying to think of something else to say. "Down here on vacation?"

"You could say that."

"Having a good time?"

"You could say that."

"You staying much longer?"

"It depends."

"I like that in a woman. Not talking much. Not saying nothing except what needs to be said." His eyes flitted to Lilah, who dropped hers, and then turned to the swimmer. "Hey, Delaware," he called out. "Finished with that pool over there yet, man? That's Delaware Brown over there, doing them laps like he's going to the Olympics."

Delaware Brown climbed out of the pool and walked slowly toward a group of beach chairs. Water beaded on his skin, and dripped off his red bikini in rivulets. He walked with a swagger, like a man who thinks he's better in bed than he is. His chest and legs were big like a heavyweight's, almost too big for his body, and there was a roughness to his angular face that made him look like he'd done some time in the ring or the joint. His eyes were a pale brown, almost hazel, and were a stark contrast with the deep molasses color of his skin. He snatched a hotel towel from the side of the chair and wiped his face and neck, then walked toward the bar.

"I'm going to get myself a drink, Sammy Lee. Jesus Christ, it's hot in this goddamn place."

"That's Delaware Brown," Sammy repeated with admiration, as if I was supposed to recognize his name. "Come on, Delilah. I'm going on in and have another drink with Delaware."

"I want—"

"Come on in with me into the bar, little lady." His hand fastened on her shoulder, and she shook it off. He dropped it to his side and walked toward the bar.

She watched him go and then gave what sounded like a sigh of resignation and turned to follow him. "Nice meeting you, Tamara Hayle with a *y*," she said over her shoulder.

"Take care of yourself now, Lilah Love," I replied, and meant it.

And that should have been the end of it. Anyone with the sense she was born with would have known that folks with names likes Delaware Brown and Delilah and Sammy Lee Love couldn't mean nothing but trouble. But I've always been a woman whose hard head seems to land her squarely on her soft behind, who starts off strolling down the right path, then turns around and heads down the wrong one. So later on when Lilah Love came back with a grin on her face and a rum punch in her hand, curiosity got the better of me and I listened to what she had to say.

"Sammy Lee and me were thinking." She paused and handed me the drink. "You probably haven't seen too much of Kingston, except what's in them guidebooks I saw you reading before. This is like our third or fourth trip down here, and we know the *real* Jamaica, what they afraid to talk about in them guidebooks. Me and Sammy Lee and Delaware Brown was going to do some hopping, club hopping that is, later on this evening, and we were wondering if you'd want to come along.

"Delaware Brown's got a pair of wheels over there back at his hotel, so we can get around easy, and he'll take us anywhere we want to go. I know you'll have a good time, girl, hanging out with me and Sammy Lee and Delaware Brown. The whole night will be on us, Tamara, on me and Sammy Lee." She tipped her head to the side begging like my son Jamal used to do. When it didn't work, she sensed it like a kid does and changed directions.

"Ain't no fun being in a city like Kingston by yourself, girl. A single woman traveling by her lonesome. And I need some company. Please help a sister out. I'm tired of being alone with these two dudes, out here all by myself. I swear, sometimes I don't think I got the sense my mama left me."

There was something in her eyes when she said that last part that I couldn't read but that touched me. *Was she afraid?* I wondered. I've always been a sucker for the fear in people's eyes.

"We're on the third floor. Room 314. Better still, meet you back here at ten?" she asked, rushing the words together. "You won't regret it."

The Jamaican twilight was beginning to turn the city pink, and I could hear the reggae pumping hard and heavy down the road.

"Okay," I finally said, and smiled agreeably. But somewhere in the back of my mind, a warning played, like the kind that used to come from my dead grandma when I was a kid.

I should have listened.

2

I should have listened to her warning about the look in those boys' eyes too. There were three of them leaning against the bar in the Stamp and Go, the hole of a club where we finally ended up. They were all about the same age as my son, all dressed in the same hooded, baggy gear that teenagers profiling "hard" like to wear—too hot for down here, but homage to the kids in the videos piped down from the States. God knows, I'd seen that look often enough on the faces of teenage boys back home: anger curled like a grimace around the lips; eyes set deep in young faces hardened by despair. Desperation reared in poverty looks the same, whether it's hanging tough in the Seth Boyden Homes in Newark or leaning against a poor man's bar in Kingston. But threats from baby gangsters were the farthest thing from my mind that night, and by the time we'd reached the Stamp and Go, the rum, the heat, and Sammy Lee's filthy mouth had dulled my instincts. I just didn't see what was coming.

The Stamp and Go was Delaware Brown's idea. Its narrow door, marked by green-and-yellow Wray and Nephew signs, led to a small room as dim and cool as a cave. The dreary blue walls were streaked with something that looked like grease, and wood peeked through the dirty linoleum that covered the floor. The room was lit by four red bulbs which cast a blood-red glaze in the darkened corners. A radio blared new hip-hop and old hits from the eighties: Debarge, Donna Summers, and Barry White brought back my youth and the dull sense of dread I feel whenever I remember it. My brother Johnny had put a hole in his head the summer of my twentieth year. There are wounds in your heart that rub sore at the least provocation, and this was mine. He's been dead nearly fifteen years, but it always takes me a minute or two to knock the memory of what happened back inside me whenever I think about him. I thought about him tonight.

The dozen or so people who were packed into the place gave us suspicious, wary glances as we entered. A stocky bartender wearing a T-shirt torn at the neck and a grin that showed too many teeth whistled as he chipped pieces off a block of ice with a nasty-looking pick. The crowd was mixed. One or two hustler types Jamaican-style decked out in dark, tight trousers, clinging jerseys, and check-me-out Carrera sunglasses sucked nervously on cigarettes. Several weary laborers leaned against the bar drinking as seriously as my father used to drink, their eyes vacant of everything but exhaustion. Three young women heavy on makeup and attitude tossed me and Lilah evil eyes, which Lilah returned with a sultry, devil-may-care toss of her head.

I'd put on an overpriced white sundress I'd treated myself to in a moment of guilt-ridden self-indulgence, which looked good against the deep bronze glow the sun had given my skin. Lilah was dressed like the kind of woman who would give a sister some grief. She'd poured herself into a tight red knit number that fit her like a tube and her face looked older and harder, even though she'd seemed vulnerable and nervous when we met in the lobby. She'd popped a small flash on top of the Minolta and began taking pictures nonstop of anything that crossed her path the whole time babbling on in the same one-sided conversational style she'd used on me poolside.

Sammy Lee was drunk and getting drunker. He'd started in on Lilah before we left the hotel, criticizing the way she was dressed: how tight her dress was, how she didn't have the sense God gave a naked jaybird, how she looked like something anybody in any bar in Kingston "could fuck if they had half a thought or half a dick." By the time we got to the Stamp and Go, his mouth had gotten as mean and dirty as any man's I'd ever heard. Delaware Brown was strangely quiet. When we walked into the club, he'd pushed ahead of us, glancing around the place nervously as if looking for somebody.

A couple of men dressed like tourists were bunched together near the teenagers at the end of the bar. One was a short blonde with round eyes and a pointed nose fringed by a mustache. A squat, black duffel bag sat on the floor next to his left foot, between him and the skinny guy on his left. With those big eyes and whiskers, he brought to mind Felix the Cat with his bag of tricks. I realized that I'd seen him earlier. He'd flown in on the same Air Jamaica flight with me—first-class— and spoke with what sounded like a German accent.

A brooding, caramel-colored brother with the beak of his white Kangol hat pulled low over his head slumped over the bar to the right of the white guy. He was a tall, hefty man, nearly six four, with a long face. His lazy, sleepy eyes watched everything and everyone; they were cold eyes, as narrow as a snake's, but fit well in his homely face. He wore tan Bermuda shorts and a white Polo T-shirt that was pulled low over his butt. With one powerful hand he held what looked like a rum and Coke gingerly, like a debutante holding her first glass of champagne. His fingers were so muscular they looked distorted as they strummed the table, keeping beat to the music.

A thin, lanky dark-skinned man with an angular, pockmarked face stood on the other side of the German, and Delaware's face lit up when he saw him. He and the man had the same angular face and hazel eyes, but the man's eyes were softer. A wide grin, the first expression save a scowl he'd worn since I met him, spread across Delaware's face as he headed toward the end of the bar to embrace him.

"Hey, man! Hey, Lacey! How you doin', man? I thought I might luck up and find you here," he squealed like an anxious kid as he moved toward him. The man named Lacey stepped back for a moment, and then gave a slight shrug of his shoulders and nod of his head as if he was being forced to accept something he didn't want to take.

"What you doin' here, brother? What the hell you doin' in this bar in the middle of West Hell?" Lacey's voice was jarring, higher than I expected it to be and squeaky like an excited kid's.

"What you think?" Delaware said, and both men laughed as if they were sharing some naughty secret.

"Let me talk to my man here for a minute. You'all go on and sit down. I'll be over there with you in a minute." Delaware said over his shoulder to Sammy Lee.

"What you been up to, boy?" Lacey said in a low, hushed voice, and his face became serious and concerned.

Delaware glanced quickly at Sammy Lee and a look I couldn't interpret passed between them.

"Nothin', man," he replied. "Not a goddamn thing."

"Don't I know you from somewhere, man?" Sammy Lee said to Lacey. "You been around somewhere I been."

"I don't think so, brother, maybe you got me mixed up with this son of a bitch here." He jammed his finger jokingly into Delaware's chest. "From the time we been knee high to a cockroach, running around together in the projects, people been telling us we look alike, man."

"Yeah, we're actually brothers. My old man was doin' his mama when his old man was at work," joked Delaware.

"You better cut that shit out, man, before I tell him whose mama was really gettin' done and where I was doin' it!" Lacey said, and he and Delaware laughed loudly and good-naturedly, as if trying to bring us into their good feelings.

"That ain't it," said Sammy Lee, with no laughter in his voice, his eyes not leaving Lacey's face. "I don't forget nobody's face unless I want to. Okay, man," he said after a minute, his lips moving into what looked like a smile. "You go on and talk to your partner for a spell and we be waiting for you." The curl of his lips piqued that cop part of me that notices those things. Lilah saw it too, and as we ordered our drinks, her eyes shifted nervously between her husband and Delaware. Suddenly she grinned, as if she'd just thought of something that would make things okay.

"I want to take some pictures!" she announced, like a little girl trying to please her daddy. "Come on, Delaware, let me take some pictures of you and your friend."

All three men glanced at her with surprise and then mild annoyance. She pulled out the Minolta, squinting as she adjusted the setting of the film. "I got to use the kind that takes them good in the dark, it's so damn dark in here," she murmured to herself. "Delaware, why did you bring us to a dark place like this? Just so you could meet your friend?"

"Hey, baby, what you doin'?" said Lacey, holding up his hand and pulling away.

"Put that damn thing away. Everybody is sick of you and that goddamn camera. Don't nobody want their picture taken in here. This ain't the kind of place you be taking somebody's picture," Sammy Lee growled low and harshly.

"I just want to capture the moment," Lilah said wistfully, sounding like a Kodak commercial. "Being here in Kingston, Jamaica, coming to this bar nobody ever heard of. Delaware meeting an old friend like that. Sammy, please leave me the hell alone." Her voice broke when she said it. His eyes narrowed but he didn't reply.

"Ain't nothing to remember," Delaware Brown said gently. "Me and Lacey maybe, but we don't need no pictures. Ain't no beach or sun or ocean in here, Lilah. And nothing you can't see in any bar in Jersey City."

"I want everybody close together. I don't want nobody outside the frame now." Delilah ignored him as she continued to try to move us together. Sammy Lee stepped between the German and the brother in the white Kangol and reached over for his drink.

"Put that damn camera away like I told you to, Delilah."

"All I got is my goddamn camera," she said, and began to shoot it furiously and defiantly. Sammy Lee's jaw went hard and tight. I thought for a moment that he was going to knock it out of her hand. Whatever the camera meant to her, it meant something different to him, and I realized that it was something that she used to defy him, the way some women use a child or best girlfriend. It was a part of her that he couldn't control or destroy. She used her camera to taunt him, and he knew it. But instead of attacking her, as I thought he might, he turned his back on her, angrily stepping away from the group and into the man in the white Kangol, who spilled his drink down his sweater and Bermuda shorts. It had the unfortunate effect of making him look like he'd just peed on himself.

"Goddamn you to hell," the man muttered as he turned to face Lilah, who had just snapped his picture. He brought up his hand to shield his face, but it was too late. I noticed that he spoke with what sounded like a British accent, a pretentious one, which surprised me because he was dressed like an American college student. The flash sparked twice, catching his angry expression.

"What did you say, man?" Sammy Lee stepped in front of his wife protectively, ready to take on the stranger in a silly display of macho possessiveness.

The man looked him up and down for a second. "Nothing, brother, nothing," he murmured, and seemed to shrink in size. That surprised me because he was bigger than Sammy Lee and could have taken him easily. He seemed cowed by the threat in Sammy Lee's voice.

"See what you did to that man with your goddamn camera?" Sammy Lee said to Delilah.

"I'll talk to you later," Delaware said to Lacey, who was watching everything that had gone on with a strange look on his angular face.

"Where you staying, man? Let me know and I'll give you a call."

"Across the way, over there in New Kingston. A place called the Bel Air, like that old car I used to drive, man. Room 207. Give me a ring. Two zero seven, same as the number my mama hit when she took us to the shore that time? Remember that man?"

"Yeah. I remember, I remember it." He paused for a moment. "I'll be in touch. Later on tonight, maybe?"

"Okay, man. You do that. Come on, Sammy, let's sit down," Delaware said, and steered him to a high card table just down from the bar, surrounded by four kitchen chairs. I glanced back at the man in the white Kangol as we settled in. He was still staring at Lilah, his eyes tightly focused on her face.

Sammy Lee Love sat down first, and Delaware Brown slid down beside him. Delilah hesitated, waiting for me to sit, and I slid across the table from Sammy Lee. She sat down next to me as her husband loudly ordered another round of drinks. He was what my father used to call an "evil drunk," the kind who gets nasty the minute that first drink takes hold of him good, throws a punch at the first person who crosses his path, and then lies down to sleep it off, snoring and farting like a fat, spoiled baby. He looked around the club and his eyes finally settled on his wife.

"Didn't I tell you not to take those goddamn pictures?"

"Shut up, Sammy Lee."

"Didn't I tell you?"

"You should be ashamed of yourself, Sammy Lee, the way you scared that poor man. You ain't nothing but a bully."

"Look at her there, Delaware. Didn't I tell you she is one stupid bitch." He grabbed Delilah's wrist, knocking her drink out of her hand and into her lap.

"Bad night for you and folks' drinks, ain't it, Sammy?" said Delaware Brown, and he winked at Delilah, who giggled. Sammy Lee ignored him and glared at his wife. "See what you made me do? She's one goddamn stupid bitch, ain't she, Delaware?"

Delaware Brown leaned back in his seat and studied him silently out of the side of his eyes as if he was getting ready to say something nasty, and then his stare turned cold.

"That's right, Sammy Lee," Lilah said. "Blame me for knocking my own drink in my lap the same way you blamed me for you bumping into that poor man at the bar. Blame me, Sammy Lee. Just like you always do. Go on and blame me for you being drunk and clumsy." She searched through her cotton tote bag for something to mop up the mess and pulled out a long red-and-white-checkered scarf, which she used to and dab at the rum as it soaked the table, her dress, and the bottom of her bag. I grabbed some slightly used Kleenex from the bottom of my brown and purple Kenya bag and helped her mop.

It was then that I noticed the burgundy-colored marks on her shoulder and upper arm shaped like somebody's big, thick fingers. My stomach twitched, but the sad part was that I halfway expected to see them.

"You okay?" I whispered. I could have been asking about the way the drink had dripped onto her lap and dress, but the shame in her eyes before she glanced down told me she knew what I was really asking about.

"Will you take these things before they get wet? I don't want nothing to get spoiled." She handed me her camera and a small but bulging quilted cotton bag. I stuffed them into my big Kenya bag and put it back down on the floor between us.

"Nigger, you ain't got no class at all," said Delaware Brown. "Blaming the girl for something you did. You married her, man. You got to learn to let the girl wear what she want to wear, do what she want to do."

"I told her not to wear that goddamn dress, fitting her so tight on her ass like it do," said Sammy Lee. "I told the girl every goddamn monkey in this place gonna be looking up her big ass."

"Shut up! Goddamn you," Delilah said. "People gonna hear you, Sammy Lee. Coming into somebody's country calling people monkeys, talking bad like that about people you don't know."

Sammy Lee looked around the room, daring anybody to take him on. "I ain't scared of no sonabitch here in this place. You know that, Delilah! I'm not scared of no sonabitch in here!"

I leaned back in my chair, took a long sip of the drink in front of me, and tried to figure out how in the hell I was going to find my way back to the hotel by myself. There had been no street signs or numbers on the buildings. Delaware Brown had driven fast and furiously through streets half paved and so narrow the car nearly grazed the sides of the wooden buildings on either side. Several thin, barefoot children had peered at us curiously as we drove past, and when we'd entered the bar an old woman who sat in a chair near the entrance, her gums black with age, her head held as high as an ancient queen, had stared at us in silence and then muttered something in a low voice that sounded like a prayer. I had no idea where I was.

Why had I gotten into this mess?

I glanced at Delilah, who gave me a weary smile of resignation, and then I knew.

She reminded me of myself. I'd been about her age when I filled the gaps left by my grief with strangers who I tried to make into friends. Those had been the years of DeWayne Curtis, my ex-husband and the father of my son Jamal. DeWayne had been no Sammy Lee Love—he had never hit me, insulted me, or brutalized me the way Sammy Lee obviously did Delilah, but DeWayne had torn me down in other ways—with his women, his indifference, and his constant lies. I had grabbed anyone who had come my way during those days, snatching anything that looked like it might bring me salvation and chase away the demons who were chewing up my soul. I sensed that same battle waging in Lilah now. Sammy Lee Love was the demon she would have to spit out.

"You want another drink, Tamara Hayle with a *y*?"

"No."

"It's on us."

"No, thank you, Lilah."

I studied her closely, trying to avoid staring at the marks on her arms, wondering where he'd put the other marks, and how often he beat her. I understood now the fear that had been in her eyes. She had sensed my strength as surely as I had sensed her weakness. Sisters of the spirit, on either end of the spectrum.

I owed whatever had brought me through my trials the rescue of another victim. So despite everything else, I knew I'd have to make sure I made time to talk to her back at the hotel. An older woman passing on some wisdom grounded in experience to a younger one—that was my responsibility. But she'd have to be ready to listen. That was the ugly truth about being as young as she was; no matter how much advice somebody wants to give you, you usually aren't ready to take it.

But first I'd have to get my butt out of here.

I glanced around the bar again, and decided my best bet for a safe getaway was the grinning bartender. He obviously knew the area and would know how I could get back to the hotel. He was bound to have some sense of responsibility for the well-being of his patrons, even in a dive like this. And I had one thing in my bag that always brought out the best in folks: American money, especially since the Jamaican dollar had just slipped to forty to one, forty Jamaican dollars to one dead president.

"What do you do for a living, Tamara Hayle? Are you a teacher? You seem like a teacher to me." Lilah's soft easy voice brought me back to my sorry situation.

I usually don't tell people that I'm a private investigator, the CEO and only employee of Hayle Investigative Services, Incorporated. I don't feel like going into my history, and it usually brings too many questions: what I do, why I do it, how I do it, how much money I make. Half the time I'm not sure how to answer them myself.

But I answered this time. "I'm a PI. A private investigator. I used to be a cop."

"A cop!" Sammy Lee Love squealed. "You mean we been sitting here drinking with a goddamn cop!"

Delaware Brown started to laugh so hard it shook his body until he started to cough. "You know how to pick 'em, Sammy Lee."

"Shit!" Sammy Lee screamed so loud several people turned around and glanced our way.

"Don't mind Sammy Lee Love. Don't let him get to you. He's just full of that word he just said, and he knows it," Delilah said.

"So what exactly do the three of you do?" I asked, annoyed as hell and, since I'd mentioned it, acting the part of the tough ex-cop now. "What business do you have in the islands, since you seem to know them so well?"

"Delaware Brown here, you might say he's one of them entrepreneurs," Sammy Lee said, now obviously recovered. "Delilah here, well, she's my wife, and she don't do too much more than that, if you know what I mean. And me, baby doll, what you say your name was— Tamara Hayle? Officer Tamara Hayle. Me, well, I guess you could say I'm in the import/export business."

"I'm an ex-cop. Ms. Hayle is fine."

"Miz Hayle, then."

"So you all met in this import/export business?"

The three exchanged glances.

"I met Sammy Lee at the track. At the Meadowlands. I used to work in the booth, and he was always winning," Delilah said.

"Yeah, I can see that your man is truly a winner." I didn't bother to disguise my sarcasm or disgust. "So what you importing/exporting, Sammy Lee Love? I'll bet it wouldn't take a rocket scientist to figure that one out."

Marijuana, I was sure of that. Mexico and Colombia were the places to go if you were in the "import/export" business for cocaine, but ganja, brown and rich and nurtured by the Jamaican sun, was the biggest unofficial cash crop going, and this was where any "entrepreneur" ready to feed the ever-growing market in the States headed. The smirk on my lips told Sammy Lee my question was more rhetorical than anything—"devilish" my grandma would call it—just to see if I could get a rise out of him.

Sammy Lee looked at me hard and then smiled. "If you didn't look so old and tired, I might could have some fun with you."

"Why you always got to be insulting somebody, Sammy Lee?" Lilah whined. "Every time I look around, you got to be saying something bad about somebody."

"If I'm so bad, why you still with me then? But then I know what you and him is waiting for." He said it with an easy grin, offhandedly, like he was joking. Delaware Brown and Lilah exchanged quick, furtive glances.

"I'm out of here," I said, bending down to reach for my Kenya bag. Nobody heard me.

"Sammy Lee, you know me and Delaware—"

Sammy Lee stood up to his full height, reached across the table, grabbed his wife by her shoulder straps, and then backhanded her twice in a fast, fluid motion that told me he'd had a lot of practice. Delilah's head jerked back and then forward, and she touched the side of her face as if she'd been burned, her eyes big with pain and fear.

"Come on back to the hotel with me, Delilah," I urged gently. "You got too much going for you to put up with something like that."

Sammy Lee sat back down and laughed in a deep, ugly rumble that started in his throat and spilled from his mouth in a growl. He turned to face Delaware Brown. "You didn't think I knew what was going on, what's up with you, did you? And I ain't talking about you putting the moves on that pussy, man. You think I'm going to go out on a bullshit tip like this, you double-crossing son of a bitch. I knowed I seen that nigger before, I know—"

But he didn't get the chance to finish.

They shot the lights out first. The room went black and there was a barrage of gunfire in rapid, brutal succession. My breath left me like somebody had slammed me against the table. I acted with my instincts then, forgetting about everyone else and everything but my own survival.

I slipped down into my chair and underneath the rickety table to the floor, curling my body into a tight ball, hovering as close to the wall as I could get. Sweat slid down my neck and breast inside my blouse. I held my breath, afraid of the sound it would make. There was another barrage of shots, too many and too rapid to count.

It was those kids—somehow I knew it—the ones who'd been leaning against the bar with nothing in their eyes but boredom and contempt. Shooting up a bar like this was a kid thing to do, the kind of thing kids do back home. Poor kids. Dumb kids. Kids who have nothing to live for but some weird take on manhood, to prove they aren't punks, to hell with anybody who gets in their way, and I thought about those lines from a hip-hop rhyme I'd heard.

When I'm called off
I got a sawed-off.
Squeeze the trigger
and bodies are hauled off.

I listened to the sound of the guns, trying to identify it. It was something small and powerful, probably a Tec-9, I'd bet on that. Nine hundred and fifty rounds per minute. Fourteen inches long. Easy to sneak into a bar under a bulky hooded sweatshirt.

I was thinking like a cop now, trying to get a peg on the weapon, analyzing the danger, trying to keep the fear out. But my body was trembling. I felt the table begin to shake, like somebody was throwing something against it.

I couldn't see anybody. Where were the others?

How long had it been? One minute? Two? Had anyone been shot?

Everything had stopped. The room was still and completely silent. I wondered for a moment if I was the only one alive. I pulled myself tighter, hiding from a danger I couldn't see. And then somebody screamed, piercing the silence like the gunfire had a moment before. I could smell the fear in the room.

"Lilah?" I whispered her name but the sound of my own voice was strange and distant.

"Lilah?"

Nobody answered.

Slowly my senses began to come back.

A scratch on my hip began to throb. I realized I must have bruised it when I'd slipped underneath the table, maybe a splinter on the edge of the seat. I'd felt nothing; terror will do that to you.

Somewhere Gladys Knight sang about that midnight train to Georgia.

I smelled a sweet metallic scent of fresh blood. I felt it sliding down my arm. I wiped it off, rubbing it off my hand onto the gritty floor.

Had I been hit?

No. There was no pain. The blood was dripping from between a crack in that cheap-ass table above me.

I saw his sandals first. The right one was wedged against my leg and moved when I did. The leather was rich and brown and crossed against his large, misshapen toes. The hand hung down limply beside me: thick fingers, buffed nails, a ruby ring with diamonds on either side. A pretty, girlish ring on a big man's brutal hand.

I shifted my body away from the foot, and he slipped under the table, the way I'd slid down earlier: legs, hips, torso, with blood oozing from the jagged tear in his chest. And finally there was the face. Sammy Lee Love's face. As dead as it could be.

3

The first time I saw a dead man's face, there was nothing left of it; a bullet had seen to that. Even though I'd known him all my life I didn't recognize him.

Why is this dead man wearing my brother's shirt?

That had been my first thought, before I let myself understand that Johnny was dead. I've made peace with death since then — respecting it and deferring to it. But I have never gotten used to it coming like it came for Sammy Lee Love and Johnny, so quick and brutal.

Getting used to people dying is one thing, making peace with evil is another. I'd run smack into it the morning I found my brother's body. Johnny wasn't evil. But the thing he'd allowed to kill him was.

My grandma had put a face on evil when we were kids. It was always perched and ready like a haint to catch you, eager to tempt and embrace you if you let it, always anxious to make a play for your soul. She preached about evil when she polished my Sunday shoes on Saturday night and burned candles to protect us from it. I'd felt its presence the morning I found my brother's body, and I felt it now as I stared into the small, dead eyes of Sammy Lee Love. In a room filled with gunfire, his wife or his friend, two of the possibly three people he trusted in the world, had grabbed the moment to stab the life out of him. *Devil gettin' his due*, was the way my grandma would have put it. *Nothing grows from evil's bloom but evil's fruits.*

"Sammy Lee," I whispered, like I expected him to answer. "Sammy Lee Love." I said his full name, solemnly, respectfully; final words spoken by the stranger he'd insulted. Then I bowed my head and said a prayer. Even Sammy Lee Love deserved some words of peace to send him to his Maker. Everybody does.

Blood from his wound had seeped down his body onto the floor and onto my dress, making a jagged border of reddish brown along the hem. I jumped out from under the table to avoid it. My knees hurt and my back and neck were stiff as I stood up; I felt like I'd been there half the night. The room was still dark, but a dim glimmer from a street-light through the open door threw a pale, eerie glow. People were moving toward it, and I could hear them whispering in fast, urgent patois.

"Hey!" I yelled, shocked by the sound of my own voice. "Hey, somebody. I need some help over here!" I tried to sound authoritative, like I used to when I was a cop, as if I was in control of a situation that had momentarily gotten out of hand. But the quiver in my voice gave me away. I sounded like some scared, helpless kid. "Somebody is hurt over here. A man is hurt bad!" I didn't say dead. People wouldn't bother coming if they knew the man was dead.

How much time had passed? Had anybody actually been shot? Had anybody called the police?

"You better leave now, sister!" a woman ordered in a tight, harsh whisper as she slipped past me toward the door. I could barely make out her face, but then realized she was one of the women who had looked me and Lilah over when we'd come into the club earlier. "This is no place to be caught now. Some white man over there under the bar spilling blood too, sister. Don't let them find you here. Go! Done is done. Be on your way!" She glanced over her shoulder as she left, and then shook her head in disbelief when I didn't move.

Sammy Lee's head had fallen limply to one side, the eyes empty, the mouth gaping. I felt sick from the smell of his blood and the look of the ragged flesh hanging from his wound. I closed my eyes, willing away the nausea. I glanced around the room again, trying to take my mind off the body slumped beside me, looking in vain for the two people who I knew wouldn't be there. They were, of course, nowhere to be seen.

Maybe he deserved it.

I thought about the sad curl of Lilah's smile, the way he'd slapped the shit out of her, the moon-shaped marks he'd left on her arm.

Yeah. I could kill a man if he laid his hands on me like that.

But could Lilah? Maybe she could. Maybe she was harder and meaner than I'd thought. Maybe the fear I thought I'd seen in those eyes was big enough to take somebody's life. Or watch somebody else take it. I had to confess that all I really knew about Delilah Love was what she'd told me, the part of her she'd let me see. Maybe I'd imagined that vulnerability I thought we shared. Or maybe she was more desperate than I'd imagined.

An opportunity had come and one of them had grabbed it. Had they done it together?

I glanced at the table where the four of us had sat: Delaware next to Sammy Lee, Lilah across from him and next to me. Delaware's arms were as thick as a skinny girl's thigh. It wouldn't take much for him to push Sammy Lee hard against his chair and jam a knife into his heart.

Done is done.

I've always had a survival instinct that snaps into place even when I don't know I'm in danger. It has kept me safe more times than I care to remember. When I listen to it, I always just scrape by—leaving the party before the razors start flying, not tasting the potato salad in which the mayonnaise has gone bad. When I don't listen to it, I end up in a mess like the one I was in tonight. It was that instinct that had pushed me under the table at the first crack of gunfire, and it was kicking in now, telling me that maybe the woman was right.

Don't let them find you here.

It would be simple enough for me to make an anonymous call from home as soon as I got back to the States. I could report to the Jamaican authorities through my lawyer (actually my good friend Jake, who is a public defender but who represents me whenever the need arises and I don't have the money, which is all the time) just what I'd seen and heard down here.

I could almost hear myself talking to the Jamaican police through Jake, sitting safe and secure in his home office back in Jersey.

I was, I would maintain, nothing more than a lonely tourist who after one too many rum punches found herself in bad company. Prior to innocently accepting an invitation to see the town. God knows, I'd never met those three people before. I had no idea who they were, where they came from, what their intentions were, or where they were going after they left Kingston.

An eyewitness to a murder?

Nooo way! Not me!

In fact, I'd actually left the table (in a manner of speaking) while and when the stabbing was taking place. I was actually a victim like everybody else in that club of random violence perpetrated by young hoodlums. I didn't hear anything, see anything, smell anything.

It would be as easy as that.

Now it was time to get my butt back to my hotel, pack my bags, sit in my room and watch BET reruns on television until morning—God knows, I was too wired to sleep. In the morning, I would check out of the hotel, go straight to the airport and head out on the first thing smoking back to Newark, for once glad as hell to see that place, talking to

```
*********************************************

        New Hanover County Library
5/26/2016 5:54:48 PM           910-798-6302

*********************************************

Automated Telephone Renewals 910-798-
                  6320

Renew Onl ne at http://www.nhclibrary.org

*********************************************


Title:        Where evil sleeps
Author:       Wesley, Valerie Wilson
Item ID:      34200004102964
Due:          6/16/2016


*********************************************
```

nobody about nothing. The hell with the days I'd paid for at the Montego Bay, somebody else could have them.

Done is done. Be on your way!

I've lived long enough to know not to look for trouble, and when it finds you, the best thing you can do sometimes is lay low until it finds somebody else. There was nothing I could do now. The woman *was* right; I should be on my way.

I tried to remember if anyone had seen me leave the hotel with the three of them. But even if they had, it wouldn't matter. Whoever was on duty at the front desk then probably wouldn't be back on until the same time tomorrow night. By the time the Jamaican cops put it together, I'd be in the Blue Demon (my son's nickname for my 1985 blue diesel Jetta) heading home on the Garden State Parkway.

And I was sure of one thing. I'd never see Delilah Love or Delaware Brown again in life. They were probably as anxious to get away from me as I was them. They both knew my name, but they also knew I was an ex-cop, so they wouldn't dare threaten me in any way. They'd also be praying their butts off that this particular ex-cop wasn't a straight-arrow ex-cop who would feel the need to share what she knew with the proper authorities. By morning, they'd both, either together or separately, be headed for the other side of the world. I only hoped I didn't run into one of them at the airport.

Sammy Lee Love was dead, and that was the end of that. Maybe he'd gotten what he deserved. Maybe this was the way things evened out. Or maybe not, but I did know one thing: Vengeance was the Lord's, not mine. Whatever happened here or was about to, I should get the hell out like everybody else.

I stooped down by the table as close to Sammy Lee Love's body as I could get without touching him and began to feel around the floor for my Kenya bag. Wherever I was going and however I ended up getting there, I needed money and my passport. I felt behind both chairs, and then on the floor underneath them, touching the rungs of both chairs and the dirty floor as I searched.

Had Sammy Lee knocked my bag out of the way when he'd slipped down to the floor?

Repulsion swept me as my hand touched his blood. I quickly wiped my hand on the sleeve of his shirt, and then snapped myself out of it, pushing back my disgust, and felt around on the floor again. I swallowed hard and closed my eyes, making myself remember what it had been like when I was a cop. I hadn't been squeamish then. I was out of practice.

Pretend you're doing something else.

That was how you beat it. I made myself search the space down from his chest, flailing around in the air and touching the sides and seat of the chairs. My arms hurt as I strained, reaching for anything I could feel.

The floor was filthy, and I could feel the grit with my fingertips. My hands grazed the chair again, and then the table leg. I leaned forward, carefully avoiding the blood that had formed a pool near my knees. I stretched forward and then swept my hand back, lightly touching the floor in a wide arc. My fingers grazed something hard, metal. I realized in the same instant that it had to be the knife, the one that had killed him. I shoved it away from me in disgust with the side of my palm. It looked almost like a jackknife, with a long curved handle of pale, mother-of-pearl green. The blade was the kind that could fold into its shaft, something you could fit into a pocket or under a jacket, but the blade was long and jagged, designed to do damage, to kill or wound.

"Shit!" I cursed out loud, yanking my hand back as if it had been burned, wiping it instinctively and repeatedly on the skirt of my dress. I pulled away from his body for an instant, rocking back on my haunches away from the table. Then I counted to ten and forced myself to take a deep breath. I edged close to his body again and got back down on my knees, squinting through the darkness for the familiar bulky shape of my Kenya bag, more determined now to find it.

But there was nothing there.

Everything I needed to get me out of this mess was in that bag: my money, the key to my room, my passport, my credit cards, my way out of here. Everything. The bag was like an extension of myself, in a weird way. I always carried that Kenya bag, and I felt naked without it. A strange sense of loss swept over me, like I'd just discovered I'd forgotten to put on a bra or some other essential piece of clothing. I got down on all fours, supported myself on one hand, squinting to see as far as I could and wildly sweeping the space around his body and the floor with the other. Another thought came then, and I felt a rush of shame at being taken in as a sucker as I realized what must be the truth.

She had taken it.

I was the vulnerable one, not Lilah Love.

Maybe she needed the money, maybe my passport or the key to my room. Maybe she'd taken it simply because her bag was in mine. Whatever it was, she had it. She had stolen my bag, and the fear I felt in the pit of my stomach turned to rage.

"Damn you, you thieving little bitch! Damn you!"

I know what you and him is waiting for. I remembered the evil glint in Sammy Lee Love's eyes as he spoke those words, and the secretive, guilty glance his wife and his friend had shared. The space was too tight for Delaware Brown to put a knife through Sammy Lee's heart without Lilah seeing it, and I'd been the only one under the table. If she would watch her husband being stabbed to death, she would damn sure steal my Kenya bag without a second thought.

The wail of police sirens is the same all over the world, and I heard it now, screaming loud and long, two, maybe three blocks away.

"Jesus Christ!" I screamed out loud, but I should have been praying. My heart had started to beat so wildly I could hear it in my ears.

Here I was, sitting on the floor of a cheap hustler's dive in the middle of Kingston, Jamaica. There was a dead man lying at my feet, I'd just put my fingerprints on the knife that killed him, and his blood was smeared in an ugly red design on the bottom of my fancy white dress. I had no identification, driver's license, passport, key to a hotel room, money, or proof even that I hadn't come here with Sammy Lee, that I wasn't his wife, that I hadn't taken the knife that lay beside him and put it through his heart. Anyone who could verify my story—from Delaware's friend Lacey to the brother in the white Kangol—had gotten out while the going was good.

I couldn't breathe for a minute, and when I finally caught my breath it stuck in the top of my throat like a choke.

What the hell am I going to do?

I wouldn't believe me if I were the cop in charge, that was for damn sure. Even if some good-hearted sheriff gave me some slack and the benefit of the doubt, it could take days to verify everything that needed verification. I could end up spending two weeks in a Jamaican jail before my best girlfriend Annie or my sister Pet or Jake, God bless him, could get the money together to fly down and get me. God knew the shape I'd be in by then. Delaware and Delilah would be long gone too, to wherever they were headed.

Defeated, I sank back against the chair, listening to the sirens approach, a sense of doom overwhelming me.

"Tamara!"

I jumped, not sure at first of what I heard, but the voice was deep and familiar.

"Tamara! Come with me!" Without seeing, I grabbed a hand and followed him out of the club, not looking forward or back, my mind empty of everything except fear. I would have followed the devil through the gates of hell to get out of that room.

But it wasn't the devil. It was Basil Dupre.

4

"I will tell you what you want to know when we get where we are going," he said.

That Basil Dupre knew what I would ask before I'd said or even thought it didn't surprise me. For as long as I'd known him, he had been walking in, through, out, and back into my life, knowing me better than I wanted him to and turning everything I took for granted upside down.

There are men who mark you for life, who make a shiver of lust rumble through the pit of your belly whenever they cross your mind. The very thought of them brings a smile to your lips in inappropriate situations: sitting piously in church, sipping tea with your best friend's mama. Men who when you think of the things you've done (or would like to) make you catch your breath and giggle in mischievous, naughty delight. For me, such a man was Basil Dupre.

He was handsome in the way black men can be: skin as smooth and rich as strong coffee; a taut, powerful body that just begged to be stroked; soft, sensual lips that seemed to pause and curl around each word they spoke. There was a singular, masculine grace in everything he did—from the way his clothes hung elegantly on his body to his voice, sweetened with the lilt of a Jamaican accent. He had a tenderness that flickered in his eyes when I least expected to see it and brought back a memory of every man I'd ever loved. But there was also a toughness about him, a fearlessness that had an ominous, dangerous edge.

I have never known a man who could charm or seduce me with so little effort. We've never managed to sleep together (my ever-nagging doubts and bad timing more than anything else), but my feeling for him defies logic, morality, and just plain common sense.

Years pass between our meetings. The first time I saw him, more than ten years ago, was in my ex-husband's living room, and the attraction between us then was so strong and immediate I tucked it away and didn't let myself think about it for a good five years. The last time I saw him still burns in my memory—a moment of mutual but unfulfilled passion in the space between the refrigerator and the table on my gritty kitchen floor. My self-control and the good sense my grandma taught me took a back seat to my hormones that particular afternoon. But all I can do when he strolls into my life is pray for the best and keep a firm hand on my drawers.

I followed him now, torn between fear of what I'd left, uncertainty about where I was going, and simple, heady delight at seeing him again. We raced around a dark sharp corner and through two narrow streets, little more than unpaved paths, and then back again to the main road and down an alley. I nearly stumbled on a large furry object that I couldn't see and didn't want to. The creature took off quickly in the opposite direction. Basil gave me his hand to steady and guide me toward a black Honda motorbike that leaned against a wall. He climbed on and nodded for me to get on behind. Hiking my bloodstained white dress high on my thighs, I climbed on, gingerly clasped my arms around his waist, and then grabbed him tightly. The bike gave a raspy, mechanical grunt and stalled. He patted it as if it were a scared cat or willful kid, whispered either a curse or a prayer, I couldn't tell which, in anxious patois, then turned the key again. It hummed to a start. We took off, my arms still tight around his waist, my eyes closed so tight I saw nothing but red.

For a full fifteen minutes, I was conscious of nothing but the lurch of the bike on the ragged, deserted road, the solid feel of his body bumping against mine, and the cool whip of the wind as it hit my face and blew through my hair. Finally I opened my eyes, squinting through the wind and the darkness that enveloped us. There was nothing for as far as I could see but the black ribbon of a road ahead of us and the palm trees that threw graceful swaying shadows against the sky. The stars and full moon seemed brighter than I remembered them being in the States. The city was behind us now, and I sucked in my breath, pulling in air that carried the deep, musty smell of the sea.

"Where are we going?" I yelled into his ear through the wind and the hum of the bike.

"Away from Kingston. Morant Bay," he yelled back, over his shoulder.

Where the hell was that?

I shifted uncomfortably on the hard wedge of the narrow seat we shared. He slammed into a bump and the bike tipped dangerously. I tightened my grasp.

"You're trembling. No danger can touch you now."

"It already has," I mumbled, more loudly than I meant to.

He glanced over his shoulder, and then back at the road, a half smile settling on his lips.

With each mile we covered, the horror of Sammy Lee Love's murder sank farther away, almost as if my mind was protecting me from so much violence taken in so quickly. I let my breath out, pulled it again, counted to ten slowly and then exhaled, pushing out my fear, like they tell you to do in magazines to release tension and calm yourself down.

How much time had passed? Fifteen minutes? Half an hour? It had been after midnight when we'd wandered into the Stamp and Go. But when had the shooting started? An hour after we'd gotten there? My mind seemed to black out details of things that had happened only a short while ago.

Basil drove faster now, turning sharply to the side of the narrow road every now and then to avoid a car or truck that sped past.

"What time is it?"

"Three, four. I don't have a watch."

"Where are we going?" I asked, then remembered that he'd told me a moment ago.

"Morant Bay. There's a beach there. It's quiet, calm, and we can talk."

The last place I wanted to go was to a beach, but I was too tired to protest, to even think. I let my head droop against him, making myself forget for a moment everything but the feel of him against me. The motor of the bike strained as he shifted into a higher speed. The night was empty of every sound except the distant chirp of insects, and it was cooler now. Pleasant. I felt myself relaxing, slowing down, the panic I'd felt only a while ago finally lulled in me.

But even now the half-formed thought that I'd buried since he'd led me out of the Stamp and Go fought its way through—that second sense that keeps me ever vigilant, even when I wish it would leave me alone. It was the thought that had first come when I saw him, and now it returned, an unwelcome intrusion. I snapped my head up and sat up straight in my seat, my back stiffening.

Why had he been there?

"I think we'd better talk, Basil." I said to him over the hum of the bike.

"What did you say?"

"I said I think we should talk."

"Let's wait until we stop," he yelled back.

"I think I ought to go back to my hotel. Back to my hotel," I repeated louder.

"What is your hotel?"

"The Montego Bay."

"Ah, yes. The Montego Bay. I have a second cousin who works there as a maid. A country girl. Mavis."

"What did you say?"

"I said my cousin Mavis works in the Montego Bay."

"How far are we from there now?"

"Too far."

"I'd like to go back. Now."

He slowed the bike and pulled over to the side of the road. For a split second I felt that spark of panic and dread that says maybe you've played some move wrong, made a fatal mistake. I wondered with a sudden, dulling anxiety if coming with Basil was a mistake—jumping from the wok into the gas jet, as Jamal would put it. Could he abandon me, leave me standing here in the middle of nowhere? He climbed off his bike to face me. I searched his face for an answer.

"I have brought you here because you may need a simple alibi, everybody there will," he said, answering my unspoken thought. "If what I think happened did, the police may ask you what you know. It is better that you say you were with me. If they question you, you can answer them truthfully about where you've been and what you've seen. Half a lie is always easier to remember than a whole one." The doubtful look in my eyes must have given me away.

"You really don't trust me. After all this time, and all that's gone between us. You still don't trust me."

"I didn't say that, Basil." He had, of course, hit it on the head. But I also realized just how dependent upon his goodwill I now was. I climbed off the bike and made an effort to smooth down my dress.

I studied him, trying to decide what was really on his mind. But Basil was, as always, inscrutable.

"I have been nothing but kind to you, Tamara, in all of the years I've known you. I've done nothing to make you suspect me of anything but the best intentions. Perhaps it is yourself you don't trust. Believe what you know, not what others have told you."

"Nobody has told me anything about you one way or the other." I knew that was a lie, even as I said it. Everybody—from my friend Annie to my ex-husband DeWayne Curtis—had something to say about the brother. I just didn't know where the truth lay.

I'd heard he'd killed a man here in Jamaica, a debt of honor to avenge his father's death, and that was why he left his country and could never come back. But here we stood, and he wasn't acting like a man who was a fugitive; he seemed to have no fear or caution. I also knew he was very smart, a man who had educated himself and taught himself how to survive. DeWayne, his ex–business partner, had sworn he was a thief and a liar. But if DeWayne said a man was honest and gave him his blessing, you'd be wise to count your fingers after you shook his hand. DeWayne putting the bad mouth on somebody amounted to an endorsement of his character. I'd seen Basil threaten a man's life, and I knew the world he lived in was one of danger and deceit, yet he had told me once that he would never let any part of that world touch me. But I wasn't sure if he was a man of his word. What he said about having a alibi provided by him made sense, though. I had to admit that despite my doubts. He was right about my needing an alibi. But I needed to know more.

"What do you know about tonight? About all that shooting? About those kids?" I asked him now. "What are you doing in Kingston?"

"I live here, Tamara. My family is here, what's left of it anyway. My roots grow deep here."

"But why are you here now?" I eyed him suspiciously. "How did you manage to walk into that place at that moment?"

"Always the cop," he said with some amusement.

"Why here and now? The last time I saw you—" I stopped, not finishing the sentence. The last time I'd seen him we'd both been in various stages of undress on my kitchen floor.

He cocked his head to one side slightly, amused. My face grew hot with embarrassment.

"Yes?"

"I don't understand why you're here, Basil. I'd heard you couldn't come back here. I'd heard—"

He shrugged. "Believe me, Tamara, not everything you've heard about me is true. Much of it, maybe, but not everything." Something I couldn't read came into his eyes.

"Okay. There are things you should know, that I'd like to tell you, that I have to tell you. But I don't want to talk here. They're not the kind of things one explains standing on the edge of the road." As if to underscore his point, a truck the size of a barn shook the ground beneath us as it hurtled past, taking the corner so sharply I jumped back to keep from getting hit. We both watched it as if it held some secret, subliminal message.

"Come." He murmured the one word as softly as if he were coaxing a shy child as he took my hand to help me back on the bike. "I'll take you where you want to go, but it's not wise to go back now. Wait awhile. At least until day."

I paused, uneasy for a moment, and then decided to put aside my doubts, for the time being anyway; I really didn't have much of a choice. So we rode on in silence, the Caribbean Sea lapping at the sand just beyond the road.

5

We turned off the main road when we got to Morant Bay, parked at the side, and picked our way down a narrow path overgrown with shrubs to the beach at the bottom of the hill. It was dark, except for the light from the full moon that had emerged from the clouds and brushed the sea and beach in a golden glow. The sand was wet where we sat down, and the dampness seeped through my dress, chilling my thighs. But the night air was warm and a soft breeze blew in off the sea.

"I used to live near that club, the place they call the Stamp and Go," Basil said after a while. "When I saw you leave your friends' car, I was headed to a place nearby to talk to some people I know about a man who is involved with my sister, a no-good brother of my friend Noel. Bad news, this boy, we call him Scratch, a name we gave him when he was a kid—he's evil, that one. But when the rudies ran out, waving their smokin' guns high, with your two friends behind them, like the devil was nipping at their heels, I knew I had to come to look for you. I know what kind of place that is."

"Do you know why those kids started shooting?"

"They were kids—rude boys, some call them. Rudies for short. Kids like you have at home. The kind of kid I was once," he added with a slight, sardonic smile. "Angry, frightened, with noplace to put my anger or my manhood."

"My brother was a kid like that before he became a cop."

"You should have seen their faces as they ran out, as scared as the ones who ran after them. They are desperate, poor enough to do anything for money. They were probably paid by someone for some other purpose, so some evil deed could be done in darkness, no doubt. But your friends? Why were they there?"

"They weren't my friends."

"The people you came with, then."

"I hardly knew them," I said offhandedly, putting as much space between me and my former drinking buddies as possible. "What I do know about them is that one of them killed the third. Sammy Lee Love."

"The man whose blood is on your dress?"

I'd almost forgotten about it until he mentioned it, the sad remainder of Sammy Lee Love bordering the bottom of my dress. My stomach turned and I thought for a moment I would be sick. "Somebody put a knife through his heart," I muttered.

"That pretty little girl in the red dress was up to no good, eh? I saw her leave with a big man, built like a fighter. So she had it in for this Sammy Lee?"

"That's the way it looks."

"I guess the dead one found out the hard way: The she-goat always look you in your face before she put her mouth in your basket." He gave a short grunt of a laugh, and I started giggling like a girl. Gallows laughter.

I stopped myself self-consciously. "I'm not laughing because the man is dead. Murder is never funny."

"Spoken like a true cop. Relax, baby. I won't hold it against you. It's good sometimes to take a serious thing and make a joke of it. It's the only thing you can do sometimes, believe me. But tell me, Tamara, how did you come to be with those three? To be drinking with people of that sort in a place like the Stamp and Go?"

"Boredom," I answered truthfully. "Boredom and too much free rum."

He shook his head teasingly, as if he was scolding me, and I told him about Wyvetta Green and the case that bought me the free ticket down, and how I'd hooked up with the threesome to see the "real" Jamaica that tourists never see.

"The 'real' Jamaica? You should have asked a 'real' Jamaican."

"I didn't know you were down here," I replied flirtatiously. "But you never answered me, Basil. What are you doing here anyway?" I asked, getting down to the question that he had yet to fully answer.

He paused before he said anything. "Watching my mother die. I put her in the ground last week." He said it without emotion. I tried to remember what I'd heard about his family, but I knew next to nothing about him. I'd heard he'd grown up poor in a rough, dirty corner of West Kingston. And once, during a late afternoon of shared intimacy, he'd told me that his youngest sister, Bettina, was dead.

"I lost my mother when I was a kid, but I know what you must be going through," I finally said.

"It was no surprise."

"She was sick?"

He took so long to answer I wasn't sure if he'd heard me, and then he muttered in a low angry voice, more to himself than to me.

"It was her spirit that killed her. Pulling herself to work in the house of that rich one, fat and lazy in his big place up on high. Beverly Hills, where the rich live well, like they do in the rich white man's city in your country. Slaving for them the way she never could for her own."

I thought about my own mother when he said that. She'd been a day worker too, when I was a kid, cleaning rich folks' homes until she was too exhausted to talk. There had been nothing left of her when she came home at night either, nothing to give us but her pain and her bone tiredness and her rage.

"They threw her out when she got too sick to haul her load. May they burn in hell for that."

"How long was she sick?"

"I been down here a month. Caring for her when she couldn't care for herself. It's not been easy."

"You're the kind of man who would do all that he could to help," I said. The look in his eyes, the slightly embarrassed glance of pain that cut too deep to talk about, made me want to say something, to offer some kind of comfort.

"You don't know what kind of man I am." He said it bluntly, almost sharply, and I was surprised by the way he'd put it, admitting more about himself in the distant, guilty look that flitted across his face than he could ever say in words.

"Why don't you tell me?"

"I don't know myself."

"What kind of man would you like to be?"

He thought for a moment.

"An honorable one, like my father," he said finally. "When a man buries his mother he wants what is left of him to pay her honor. And I have not been an honorable man."

I was touched by the honesty of this self-revelation, but I'm what my grandma used to call a "doubtin' woman," always holding something in reserve, especially when it comes to Basil Dupre. I had caught him at his most vulnerable, which was also his most appealing, and I'm enough of a cynic to know that it probably wouldn't last. Still, sadness shadowed his eyes in a way I couldn't remember seeing before.

"I don't know why I'm telling you this. I have no right to burden you. After tonight. After all that has happened to you. I will take you back soon wherever you want to go."

"I'm not worried."

"There is no one else I can talk to about it," he continued, as if making an excuse for his openness. "It was hard those last months. Harder than anything I've known in my life."

"What about your sisters? The other women in your family? The women in your life?" I added, admitting to myself that I was digging as I tacked on that last part about the women in his life. I knew enough about Basil to assume that he wasn't down here in his native land all by his lonesome, as Lilah Love would put it. I also suspected that no matter how much he loved his dying mother, he would probably consider caring for her women's work.

"I don't worry women with my woes, but I forget about you American women. How you expect a man to share every bit of trouble traveling in his soul." He said it with a reluctant, teasing smile, which I found myself returning. "I am my father's only son. The only male cousin alive, and it was my responsibility to care for her," he added, lifting his head slightly with pride or arrogance, depending upon how you wanted to see it. "I have no ties and some money. The women in my family work as hard and long as my mother once did. Most of my sisters have their own children now, their own men, their own worries. They are decent women, my sisters, strong women—except, of course, for the youngest," he added with a long, disgusted shake of his head. "Bettina. The greedy little one who cares for no one but herself and feels nothing beyond her own pleasure."

And with that simple statement, everything between us changed.

I've never been able to abide a lying man. Lies flew out of my ex-husband's mouth like spit, and by the time I left him, I'd had enough of them to last me a lifetime. White lies. Nasty lies. Lies meant to flatter or to cheat. I'm sad to admit that I don't think there's enough grace left in my heart to cut some poor fool any slack when it comes to lying. I can't forgive easily anymore, which is one of the things DeWayne Curtis took from me, my sense of trust. I don't let many men close enough to me to remind me that I've lost it.

Basil had lied to me. He'd told me that his sister Bettina was dead. He'd told me that the first time I'd been to his place back in Jersey. She had died, he'd said, because of my ex-husband DeWayne Curtis, seduced by both his drugs and his substantial charms. There had been the glimmer of tears in his eyes when he'd explained it to me that afternoon, and I'd glimpsed a piece of him that few other women had seen. Or so I'd thought. It was the first time I knew there was more to him than the simple physical appeal that drew me to him like a magnet, and I'd shared that soft part of myself, my own unresolved grief over Johnny and my own loneliness. I made the decision to make love with him that night (one that gets harder to make, the older I get), and only circumstance and bad timing had kept me from his bed.

Why had he lied to me about his sister's death?

Surely it was more than just a simple attempt to play on my sympathy and get into my pants. The man had to have more to him than that. But it wouldn't be the first time somebody had used a sad tale to get something he or she wanted from me. I always seem to be taken in by folks, be it DeWayne Curtis or Delilah Love or Basil Dupre.

I walked away from him toward the water saying nothing, unsure of my voice. I'd slipped off my shoes earlier, and the water sprayed my feet and ankles with cold, sandy foam. I focused on the sea, how the coming daylight had begun to streak the sky pink, and the way the light sparkled in tiny waves and ripples on the water. I heard his footsteps crunch in the wet sand behind me, and I turned to confront him.

"You don't remember, do you?" I said it without bitterness but with a smirk on my lips, like you have when you tease a kid caught in his own clever tall tale.

"What don't I remember?"

"About Bettina. What you told me about your poor dead sister, the one who died a junkie whore. The one you told me about that last time we saw each other, at your place, back in Jersey. Don't you remember? But she's alive, isn't she? And I don't understand why you would lie to me about something as serious as that. I just don't get it." I cleared my throat and forced the adult—the strong, not-to-be-messed-with sister—to hide the whine in my voice that made me sound like a disappointed kid.

"Ah, Bettina." He blew his breath out in a long, steady stream, collecting his thoughts or getting ready to lie again—I honestly wasn't sure. "I should have told you the truth, but of course I wasn't sure of it myself then. You must first understand what we put into her, all of us. To grow up like we did. She was the best of everything we had, protecting her after my father was killed. She was the apple of his eye. And of mine.

"It was as I told you that first time, that time in my place in Jersey. She came to the States at my behest. Got involved with your husband."

"Ex-husband."

"Your ex-husband and with drugs in that order. And sold herself, for the drugs that she needed, and then later simply for the money that she did not."

He glanced at me, measuring my reaction, and then dropped his eyes in shame.

"You don't understand the pride we had in her. How we revered her. I spoke of my mother's death. Bettina tossed everything she honored in her face. For a man to do what he must to survive is one thing. For a woman to whore for money and pleasure puts her beyond my love. Even my sister, as much as I loved her. She was dead to me, and I mourned her. It was as if something had got hold of her, taken her from us. I couldn't forgive her for it. Not then, anyway. I don't expect you to understand."

"And now, she's come back to life? When you need her to prove a point as you did that first time," I said, outrage marking my every word. "You're forgetting and forgiving too easily."

"It wasn't easy. I had to—" He stopped abruptly, cautiously, like someone afraid of giving up a secret to someone he has suddenly realized he can't trust. "I've told you the truth now."

"Is that so?"

"I'm not in the habit of begging a woman to believe me when I have told her the truth."

"I'm not in the habit of believing a truth that changes on a whim."

"A whim? Think what you will," he replied, his eyes flashing with anger.

"I intend to. And you were right, Basil. You are not an honorable man."

"You are fortunate to be so sure of your own goodness that you can judge others with so much certainty. It's day now. I'll take you back to your hotel."

"Let's go then," I agreed, more angry than I cared to show him, my tone as curt as his.

When it comes to men, I know when to cut my losses, when I've reached the moment that tells me lust has gone sour. So when Basil touched that space between my ear and my neck, lingering with his fingertips, and a tiny thrill spun its way cruelly down my spine, I shook his hand off like an annoying mosquito. His eyes changed then, and a coldness settled into them.

Without speaking, we walked up the hill to where the bike was parked, the silence between us tense and uncomfortable. It wasn't fully day yet, but buses were rumbling by, loaded with travelers and boxes heading to the big city, and the closer we got to Kingston, the denser the air seemed to grow with fumes, heat, and city smells, and the sun, already shining brightly, felt harsh on the top of my head.

We traveled back faster than we'd come, and I focused on what was to come, about my next move once I got back to the Montego Bay. I'd call the embassy, I decided, and report my passport missing, call Annie or Jake to get some money, and then try to get home. Everything suddenly seemed clear and manageable. It was as if daybreak had literally spread light on my problems. And what was Basil Dupre to me?

I've always chosen my hard-won self-respect over a possibly delightful roll in the sheets, that was one thing I'd learned over the years. I come first. Me and my son, not the possibility of what could be. A man who will lie is capable of anything. I'd learned that lesson hard, and I wasn't about to be taught it again.

The ride back was bumpy, but I managed to stay on the bike by holding on to Basil's blue jersey and the seat of the bike rather than his waist. When he pulled to a stop, I quickly hopped off.

"Thank you," I said in a formal tone. "For everything," I added. The man had come to my rescue, after all. I walked toward the hotel, my head held high, hips snapping. Then I thought about my keys and cursed out loud.

"What's wrong?"

"My goddamn keys," I mumbled.

"Do you want me to get my cousin Mavis? She can get you into your room."

"If you don't mind."

"I asked you. Why would I mind?"

Without waiting for an answer, he strode into a side entrance of the Montego Bay and came back with a twig of a young woman in a pale pink maid's uniform, who gave me a quick easy smile.

"This is a lady I know from the States," he said tersely, by way of an introduction. Mavis took my hand and held it a moment between her soft small ones. "How do you do?" she said briskly and properly. If she noticed the blood on my dress, she was too polite to mention it. Her doe eyes fell on her second cousin, waiting for him to explain.

"She can get you into your room," he said to me, and then muttered something back to her in rapid-fire patois to which she replied in kind. He glanced at me again.

"Despite how you feel . . ." He didn't finish the sentence. He jotted down a number on a bent card he took from his wallet. "Here, in case you need it," he said, handing the card to me. I folded it into my hand without looking at it.

"I won't need it."

He shrugged. "Suit yourself."

"Come with me, miss" Mavis said, leading me forward. "There is a back way up to the rooms, through another entrance."

"I'm sorry that things have turned out so badly," Basil said, his eyes softening.

"It be's that way sometimes," I said, with what I hoped was a devil-may-care shrug.

"Before she died, my mother—" He stopped in midsentence, as if trying to figure out a way to continue. But I cut him off.

"Is she really dead or will she be making another appearance?" I asked, putting a nasty twist on each word as I spoke it. Mavis slapped her fingers over her open mouth in astonishment. I regretted the words the moment I saw the look in Basil's eyes.

"What sorrow has made your heart grow so hard, Tamara Hayle?" he asked. Without waiting for an answer, he climbed on his bike and shot down the road without a backward glance. I was swept for a moment with a sense of regret so deep it was almost physical, but I tucked it where I couldn't feel it and stole into the Montego Bay behind his second cousin.

6

After Mavis closed the door, I stripped off my dress, dirty now with sand as well as Sammy Lee Love's blood, and dropped down on the floor. They had given me an extra room key when I'd checked in, and I searched for it, sighing with relief when I found it. But the horror of the night still played back in my head, and with it came an overwhelming sense of dread that I couldn't blot out. The more I thought about my nasty parting crack to Basil regarding the death of his mother, the worse I felt, so I tried to put that out of my mind too. His motorbike had put a whipping on my tailbone, and guilt was all I needed on top of dread and my sore butt.

I tried to think about my son Jamal, about his laughter and the wisecracks he'd make about this vacation from hell, but all I could think of were those three boys at the Stamp and Go—each of them some poor mother's son—and anxiety about my son broke through everything else I was feeling. I considered calling him, but I knew it was too early; I'd try later on.

I thought about taking a shower, making those calls to the embassy, tossing down a couple of Advils, but it seemed like too much effort. I put my head down on the damp, sour-smelling pillow, and fell asleep before I knew my eyes were closed, deaf to everything but the dull, comforting hum of the air conditioner and the high-pitched screams of some spoiled kid down the hall.

The knocking on my door started in the middle of a nightmare. It was a crazy, ragged dream filled with loud disco tunes I couldn't recognize and booming gunfire. A strange, sorrowful Johnny turned into Basil, who turned back into Johnny with a bullet through his forehead, scowling at me like the waiter who had brought me that weak excuse for a cup of coffee I'd had at breakfast. Somebody I couldn't see but was sure I knew was knocking on the table, loudly, then softly, trying to get my attention as the scowl on Johnny's face got deeper and uglier as the knocking intensified.

I opened my eyes and looked around the room, squinting as I adjusted to the harsh morning sunlight. The air conditioner had gone out again, and I could feel the sweat dripping down my face and back. It took me a minute to remember where I was, and another to chase away that dream and recall what had happened last night.

When the knocking started again, I listened for a moment, my stomach flipping with each thump. It was the cops, I was sure of it, and there wasn't a damn thing I could do about it. I glanced down at my dress lying in a heap on the floor beside the bed, wondered if I had time to stuff it in my suitcase, and realized in the same moment that my suitcase would be the first place they'd look.

I swallowed hard, my mind racing through my options as I tried to come up with some half-assed sensible excuse as to why Sammy Lee's blood had formed a border at the bottom of my dress. I tried to remember the name of the beach where Basil had taken me, but came up blank. I wondered if they'd give me one call, like they're supposed to give you in the States, and who I should make it to. The embassy? My sister Pet? My girlfriend Annie? I took a deep breath, trying to grab hold of my mind.

"Tamara!" Her voice came in a loud, harsh stage whisper, as if she was standing close to the door. I stopped, my breath stuck in my throat.

"Tamara, it's me. Let me in. Please."

"Lilah?"

"Yeah! Sammy Lee is dead!"

"Tell me something I don't already know," I muttered. *What the hell was she doing here?*

"Delaware Brown killed him. Delaware killed my husband."

I moved toward the door, cautiously. "Are you okay?" I asked, wondering if she'd risk being here if she'd had anything to do with it, and feeling sudden concern for her as I thought about Sammy Lee's face, the dead look in his eyes.

"Yeah. I'm fine." There was no panic in her voice; she sounded almost lighthearted.

"Where the hell is my Kenya bag?" I reached for for something concrete, something I knew for sure.

"Is that all you're worried about, your goddamn pocketbook? It's over Delaware Brown's."

"You watched that man kill your husband, and then you stole my bag!" I screamed out in blunt accusation, finally getting my thoughts together. But I felt bad about mentioning Sammy Lee's death in the same context as the loss of my Kenya bag. "You thieving, murdering little bitch!" I tacked on in frustration.

What the hell was she up to? What was she doing back here?

"Stop and listen to me, Tamara. I got to talk to you about Delaware Brown. Please let me in."

His name sent a chill through me. *Was she alone?* I wondered. *Was Delaware Brown standing beside her, ready to shove in the door when I opened it? Had I underestimated my "juice" as a cop?* I was the only living witness to the fact that one of them had shoved that blade through Sammy Lee's heart. *Were they going to deal with me the same way they took care of him?*

I looked around the room for a weapon, and my eyes settled on the fake brass lamp on top of the night table. It wasn't much but I could haul it hard against somebody's head if he or she got too close. I grabbed the base and pulled, but it was glued tightly to the surface, discouraging any hotel guest from taking home a souvenir.

"Goddamn cheap-ass hotel!" I muttered.

I glanced back at the door and realized the security chain was off. I'd been so tired I'd forgotten to put it on after Mavis left. I moved back to the door, slipped it on, and peered at Lilah through the peephole.

She was wearing the same bright red tube dress she'd had on last night, but its twisted wrinkles told me she might have slept in it. Her hair hadn't been combed and her makeup was smeared in plum-red streaks down her cheeks and black circles under her eyes. She looked small and distorted, like some wizened, ugly little kid. She banged on the door again.

"We got to talk. Let me in. We got to talk."

"Get away from that door before I call the police."

"You don't want to be calling no cops any more than I want you calling them." Her little-girl voice took on a desperate but sneaky edge. "Think about it."

"Leave my bag outside the door and get away from my door."

"I don't have your goddamn bag," she snapped. "I told you it was over Delaware Brown's. I told you we got to talk, now. Please, Tamara. I'm afraid he'll kill me, too." There was a scared pleading in her voice as she whispered the last part.

"Delaware Brown?"

She paused. "You saw what he did to Sammy Lee Love. God-damn it, Tamara. You were there! You saw what happened." She started to cry, a soft sniveling sob that wasn't totally convincing.

"Are you by yourself?"

"Look out the hole. There's nobody here but me by myself. Please let me in. Please."

I looked again, and then pulled on a Howard University T-shirt that I'd thrown into my bag in lieu of a nightgown. I opened the door as far as the chain would permit, which allowed me to see to the side and back of her.

"I've got to tell you this, Lilah, because it's something you should know," I said in a tough-gal, cop voice as I glared into her mascara-smudged eyes. "I'm strapped. I have a .32 right here in my right hand, so if you try any mess, you or your partner Delaware Brown, your ass is mine. Do you hear me, your ass is mine."

She hesitated and then her voice broke with emotion as she cast her eyes upward. "Oh, thank God. Thank you, Mama, for looking out for your child! Thank you, Jesus. Thank God, Tamara Hayle, you got your gun! You got your gun! I knew you were a smart lady the minute I saw you. I knew you had it together!"

I shook my head in disbelief. "So what do you want to talk about?"

"What happened last night."

"I know what happened last night."

"Getting back your property." She paused for emphasis. "And some property that should belong to me."

I took another look through the peephole, reasonably convinced now that she was by herself, and opened the door. She stepped in quickly, glanced behind her and around the corner, and I slammed the door behind her. She looked around the room suspiciously.

"Where's your gun?"

"I was lying."

"You were lying? You mean you don't have a gun?"

"That's what I said."

"Oh, Jesus," she sighed, looking desperate. "That was really below you, Tamara, getting my hopes up like that, saying you had a gun when you didn't," she muttered, bugging her eyes in disgust. "What are we going to do now?"

"We're not going to do nothing. Last time I saw you, Lilah, you were sitting across the table from a man who ended up with a knife through his heart. You're lucky you're in here at all because I got to tell you, sis, you're still a suspect as far as I'm concerned."

"I didn't have nothing to do with it!" Her eyes got wide. "I told you, Delaware Brown killed Sammy. You think I could have had something to do with Sammy Lee's death, Tamara? You think I'd kill my own husband like that? You think—"

"Save it for the judge."

She winced very slightly, and her eyes dropped down to her feet. "I know you don't think too much of me, but you've got to believe me. I didn't know he was going to kill Sammy Lee like that. I didn't know he would do it like that. I didn't even know he had a knife, Tamara. I didn't know he had a knife."

"I'm not convinced, Lilah."

She stared at me blankly.

"Why don't you tell me what you're really doing outside my door?"

"I told you, I had to talk to you."

"Where are you coming from?"

"From Delaware Brown. Delaware Brown's." She repeated his name a second time, as if saying it disoriented her.

My face must have revealed what I was thinking, because her words came out then in a rush of explanation.

"Goddamn it, Tamara. None of this makes any sense to me, either. Can't you see that? None of this makes any sense. I just saw Sammy Lee killed, stabbed before my very eyes by this man I been, well, I been with for—oh, God! Oh, God!" She covered her face with her hands and I watched her for a minute or two crying in frustration, not saying anything. "Don't you think I feel bad. I just lost my . . . my husband!"

"So you're scared of Delaware Brown now?" I asked, pointedly ignoring the mess about her losing her husband.

She paused, and then she closed and opened her eyes, and then took a deep breath. "I told you that."

"But you just came from his place. Why don't you explain that to me. What were you doing over there?"

"What do you think?"

"So you weren't scared he was going to cut your throat when you were lying there with your legs open?"

She looked startled for a minute, her eyes big and her mouth slightly open, and then she started to cry again, snot puffing off the tip of her nose, tears staining the remaining makeup on her face. "I didn't know it was going to be like that."

"What was going to be like what?"

"I didn't know he was going to do it, kill Sammy Lee like that."

"Lilah," I said, sick and tired of her carrying on. "I let you in my damn room—show me the courtesy of telling me the truth. All the truth."

She paused for a moment, inhaled, exhaled, and then nodded that she would.

"So you and Delaware Brown definitely had something going and you knew he was going to kill Sammy Lee?" I asked, knowing the answer but not sure if she knew I did. "And Sammy Lee knew about your thing with his boy?"

"That's what he said, didn't he?" she muttered quietly.

"Is that why you all decided to kill him?"

"We didn't decide it. He just did it. We'd talked about it once or twice. But Sammy Lee was an ugly, ornery son of a bitch. You saw that, Tamara. You saw it!"

She held out her arm to show me the marks that still bruised her skin. "I could show you things like that all over my body, Tamara." She spoke in a hoarse, frightened whisper that chilled me to my bones. "Way up on my thighs where he didn't think nobody could see them. On my back, on my butt, under my arm where he whipped me with his belt, Tamara. I was scared to sleep sometimes, for what he'd wake me up to."

Suddenly she began to tremble violently, and as I watched her I realized that I'd never seen a person shake like that before. I put my hand on her to steady her, and we sat down on the bed. She stared at my dress crumpled up at her feet, looked across the room and then back at me, a scared, lost-girl look in her eyes.

"Lilah, he's dead, girl. The man's dead now. He can never lay a hand on you again. But listen to me, here you are now, sitting up here in my hotel room, just coming from having spent the night with another man just like him. Don't you get it? Can't you see that pattern?" I realized as I spoke that I was about to have the conversation with her that I promised I'd have in the Stamp and Go, the one I owed her, the one somebody should have had with me. "Here you are knocking at my door running from some man who you know killed your husband. Why? Why are you doing this? I don't think you're a bad person. I've got what my grandma used to call a sixth sense about you, which is probably why I was hanging out with you all in the first place, but you got to get yourself together, girl! Men like Delaware Brown and Sammy Lee Love are not what you need in your life. You're too young to be messing up like this."

"You don't think I know that now. I just told you I wanted to get away."

"What were you doing spending the night with him in the first place? After he killed your husband!" Saying it out loud made me realize how absurd and crazy the whole mess was, and I shook my head in amazement.

She shrugged with an empty, forlorn movement of her shoulders.

"You want to know how it started?" She stretched the words out like she was tired, dropped her head back dramatically as she spoke, and then picked it back up to face me. "The whole thing, from the beginning?"

"Yeah. Maybe you should tell me."

"I just didn't want to end up like those other women I've seen all my life. The ones whose life ain't nothing. Who start off cute, dressing nice, thinking life's going to bring them nothing but good, and end up with some fool who don't do nothing but give them grief and babies," she said after a minute. "I just didn't want to end up like my mama did, if you want to know the truth. And that brought me to Sammy Lee Love."

"Sammy Lee Love was your way out?" I asked incredulously.

"You don't know him like he was then," she said, her eyes suddenly widening with what looked like wonder. "He looked good then, Tamara, and he dressed good, too. He drove himself one of them big old Lincolns. It wasn't new but it was baaad, girl—big and black and phat. He used to come to where I worked, at that track, and think nothing at all about laying down five, six hundred dollars for them trotters, and he didn't care nothing about whether he won or lost. He just seemed to like to play the game. And I thought to myself, *I want me a man like that!*"

"How old were you then?"

"Old enough to know what I didn't want."

"So he started beating you right around the time he started giving you presents?" I asked, tossing in what I knew about men who batter women, what I'd seen when I'd been on the force, what I'd heard and read. It was a cycle, the battering and then the gifts to show they were ashamed and wanted to be forgiven, and then the battering to show that they weren't all that ashamed, and they didn't give a damn about forgiveness or anything else. The fists, the finery, the fists.

"How do you know about that?"

"And you put up with it because you figured what were a few taps to get what he was giving. So when did Delaware Brown come into it?"

She looked at me and her eyes narrowed, like a teenager challenging her mama. "You think you know just about everything, don't you?"

"More than you."

"Not enough to keep away from the three of us."

"You're right on that one." She tossed me a "Gotcha!" smile and a wink.

"So you started off with Sammy Lee Love. How did you hook up with Delaware Brown? Weren't you scared?"

"I'm not scared of too much anymore," she said, with a simple honesty that made me take her at her word. "Sammy Lee was always talking about this dude Delaware Brown. Delaware Brown this. Delaware Brown that. Me and Delaware going to do this or do that or make some bucks, me and Delaware Brown. So it was just natural that I would want to meet this Mr. Delaware Brown."

"There's a big step from meeting to fucking."

"You don't got to be so crude."

"Baby, crude is when you sleep with the dude who just put a dagger through your old man's heart. Crude is convincing some poor do-gooding sister like myself to feel sorry for your sorry behind. Crude—"

"All right. I get the point. But it just happened," she said, with a graceful little wave of her hand. "I met him. We liked each other. We started getting together every now and then. Sammy Lee started banging me around in front of him, and it got on his nerves. We talked about how it would be if Sammy Lee was dead, but I didn't think he was actually going to kill him. They were friends. Sammy Lee was my husband.

"I just feel like I got caught up in their mess, Tamara. I don't know if you can understand that or not, you look like you've always had it together, so none of this probably means shit to you, but I just got caught up in their mess."

"And you tried to get *me* caught up in their mess."

"That was Sammy Lee's idea. But you guessed what we were doing. I knew you was smarter than him."

"Well, if I'd been so smart, I would have kept my butt in this hotel room." I said, more to myself than to her. "And you all were buying and selling drugs. Marijuana? Very small-time, I'll bet."

"It was about to get bigger. Much much bigger," she said, like she was proud of it. "Bigger than any of us thought it would get. And Sammy had been watching you for a couple of days. He's good at that." She paused, catching herself. "*Was* good at that, watching somebody so they don't know they being watched. And when you first checked in, he knew you might be what we needed—what he needed. So he says to me to come over and talk to you and get to know you."

"What did you need me for?"

"He wanted to get somebody to carry shit, you know, be a courier? I guess that's what they call them. Carry cash, payoffs, anything we needed carried, since things were about to get bigger. Somebody from around Newark or Jersey who we could be in touch with easy. Some single lady who was by herself and looked like she could use some bucks. You looked like you fit the bill."

I grimaced.

"When he saw you checkin' out Delaware, like you were doing while he was swimming, like you had something cozy on your mind, he told me to go make my move."

"And you made it?"

"Right. You wearing that suit made it easy. Where did you get it anyway? I got mine in the Short Hills Mall. I tried to wait for it to go on sale but—"

"And I fell for it," I interrupted her.

"Right."

"And then?"

"And then you said you were a cop."

"Ex-cop."

"So we knew the whole thing had gone down the toilet."

We sat there for a while, neither of us saying much, her tired from the telling, me from the listening. I thought for a minute about calling the police—thought hard about it. It would be easy for them to find out the truth of the matter—about Delaware Brown, Sammy Lee Love, and this soft-voiced, hard-edged little sister. I looked at her, waiting for an answer, watching her as she let her head drop down to her chest and inhaled and exhaled again like an old woman who has seen too many deaths.

I went into the bathroom, washed out the toothbrush glass with Neutrogena soap and hot water, and then brought her a glass of water. She drank it quickly, not thinking about it.

"So after he killed Sammy Lee, what happened?" I asked, when she'd gotten down to the bottom of the glass, anxious to hear the end of the story.

"He said, 'Come on, baby, let's go,' that's all. It happened so quick I can hardly remember it." She studied the glass like she was surprised the water was gone. "I wasn't even sure he had done it, he did it so fast and all. Whoever was doing that shooting had stopped. Delaware did it when the lights were out. Folks were leaving. It was dark but there was enough light coming in from the door to see Sammy Lee. I remember wondering how he could've died so fast, and I reached out for him, wondering if he was still alive, but then Delaware kept saying come on, Lilah, come on now, baby, and he grabbed at me, grabbed my hand. I looked around for you for a minute, and then I thought about my money. My mama used to say never leave a place with a man unless you got your own money. So I grabbed that bag, 'cause that was where the money was. I looked for you, though. Where did you go?"

"Under the table."

"Word? The table where we were at?"

"Yeah. I jumped under it when the shooting started."

She tilted her head for a minute, like she was thinking about it. "That was smart," she said with a look of admiration, and then her eyes dropped down again. "I didn't even know he had a knife on him, Tamara."

"So you left there, went back to his hotel?"

"Drove back. He has a car, remember? How did you get back?"

"Never mind."

"He just started cussing, the only time I heard a man cuss worse than Sammy Lee. I didn't say nothing. Not even when we got back. Not even when we got into bed. I just kept my mouth closed. And my legs, too, if that's what you're thinking." She added the last bit with a demure toss of her head.

"Why didn't you make him bring you back here?"

"Back to this place? Now that would be stupid. The cops might be here, might have figured out who Sammy was and where we stayed. I haven't been anywhere near our room since I left it last night. Delaware's room is nice. Nicer than this place. I was scared to leave anyway. Delaware was acting so strange and shit, I was afraid to say anything or do anything that might make him mad at me."

"Killing somebody like that does tend to bring out the worst in somebody," I said dryly. "So when did you get yourself together enough to leave?"

"Somebody came by. They talked for a while, and then the guy left, and Delaware got agitated and mad all over again, and I got out of there fast. I got some money out of his wallet and came back here." She rushed the words together, avoiding my eyes, focusing on the wall behind me, and I sensed she was lying.

"Who came by?"

"Hell if I know. I was in the bedroom."

"The bedroom! How did you know somebody came by then?"

"I heard the bell ring."

"He has a bell on his hotel room door?"

"Knocker? Bell? I don't know, Tamara! Please stop yelling at me.

I just saw my boyfriend kill my husband. Ain't that worth some kind of slack? Why don't you give me a fucking break!"

"So you didn't see him then?

"No! I told you that! When I came out, whoever it was, was gone. I wanted to ask you something, Tamara," she added, facing me now, her eyes holding mine tight. "I know you want your bag back with your passport and key and everything else, and I wanted to ask you if you would go back over there with me, and get that back. And the money, too, that they owe me. The money," she added quickly, and repeated it like she wasn't sure that I'd heard it. "I don't really give a shit about any of them or what happens to them. All I care about is that money."

"Money? What money?"

"Money they got stashed over there."

That was one thing I was sure she was telling the truth about. It always ends up being about money. I should have known that. The money was why she'd shown up banging on my door with tears in her eyes. I stood up and walked over to the door to slip on the chain I'd taken off, more for something to do while I was thinking than anything else.

"You said you were a PI, right? That's a private investigator?"

I didn't answer, cursing to myself—mentioning what I did for a living always ended up getting me in trouble.

"I need somebody to go over there with me. To watch out. I want to get the money. It's over Delaware's, and I want my share. I worked hard for it. I took the risk for it. I want it," she added, like a spoiled kid asking for her share of ice cream. "I know where it is too. I can find it fast." She glanced up at me, something in her eyes I couldn't interpret, and then she changed it, adding quickly, "I kind of know where it is. You might still have to help me look."

"That's not the kind of stuff I do," I said. "Retrieving money for drug dealers."

She thought for a minute before she spoke. "I ain't no drug dealer.

They were. I'm not. What about your stuff? Do you want to get out of this country without cops crawling all over your ass? We need each other. If we go over there together, it's two against one. He won't be able to hurt either of us. Will you come with me?"

I waited for her to run the "help a sister out" business on me again, but all that came was a sigh that seemed to go through her.

"You know it's all about the money, you're smart enough to know that," she said after a minute, in a quiet, matter-of-fact voice with a look of sincerity that cut through all my doubt. "It belongs to me, Tamara. Every damn bit of it with interest paid."

"How do you figure that? Since you're not a drug dealer?" I asked, with a hint of sarcasm coloring my words. She glanced back at me, her eyes looking hurt.

"For what I gave Sammy Lee and what he took," she said. "Not just physical but money, cash. I staked him, Tamara, because he told me it would pay off big, and it did sometimes, but just nickel-and-dime big, not what I gave him. I gave him money that was mine in the be-ginning, when he said he was down on his luck. It wasn't a lot of money, but it was all I had. It was enough to change his losing streak, enough to help him get in tight with Delaware so they could turn it into some big cash. It was money from a big old pretty diamond that used to belong to my mother. Money I earned and saved," she said, her voice breaking, as she glanced up at me. "I staked that foul son of a bitch so many times in so many ways I can't even recall it all. It wasn't much money when I gave it to him, but it has got itself some interest on it now. It's got itself some interest."

"How much money did they leave in the room?"

"At least six. That's what it looked like. That's what I could see."

"Six hundred? Six thousand?"

"Six figures."

"Damn!" I said despite myself.

"I'll give you thirty thousand of it if I can get some of it back, that's fair. If there's a lot there, I'll only take what's mine, and I'll give you what you deserve too," she said, and then her voice went low.

"I will hate him until I'm old and moldy in my grave, 'cause I know when I'm laid out on the undertakers's table, all stretched out with nothing left of me but my soul, Sammy Lee's marks are still going to be on my body. He whacked me around so much, made me feel so bad about myself that he'll have the last say about my life. His words are written all over top of me, Tamara. He wrote it with them big, ugly hands, and that's the truth of it."

"No, that's not the truth of it, Lilah. Nobody can have the last say about your life but you."

"And that's why I need that money," she said with sudden, firm certainty. "That money is going to mean my life. You said that before about my being too young—well, I *am* too young. Damn, here I am only twenty-one, and I'm talking about a new start. Ain't that somethin'? And when I get that money, that's what I'm going to get. Tamara, you won't see nothing but the steam off my butt because I'm heading out fast, so if you want what's yours, you better come on with me now."

I tossed it around for a minute or two, the pros and cons of helping Lilah Love. I'm not going to lie about it, I've never been one who could afford to turn down money, even if it might have a little shadow hovering around the edges. A dollar is a dollar, and I scuffle for every dime I make. I have health insurance bills that break my butt every other month, and a teenage son who is headed for college and will probably *not* get an academic scholarship. I am, always have been, and will always be where the buck stops for my son—me and me alone. Thirty grand would cover two, maybe three years of anywhere he wanted to go; it would soften those sharp edges that always seem to cut into my life. Give me some breathing room for a couple of years. It was a hell of a lot of money for a couple of hours' work—more than I would see in ten years of Sundays. And the three of them owed me something for this mess anyway. "I don't want no shit, Lilah," I said quietly.

"Delaware won't give us no problem. I promise you that," she said, and a hint of something passed over her eyes, a shadow I didn't quite understand that made me cock my head and look at her out the side of my eye, but she kept on talking. "I just need you for backup if I need it. For protection."

"Against Delaware Brown?"

She nodded without saying anything, her eyes focused on a place behind my head I couldn't see. I looked her up and down, assessing her as I'd been doing every minute since she had strolled into my life along with her battering husband and murdering boyfriend.

"I don't want no shit," I repeated, with a warning, kick-ass gleam in my eye.

She gave me a shrug like she only half heard me. "You ready to get started?"

Without saying anything, I slipped on some jeans, shoved the extra room key into my pocket, and put on a pair of sunglasses and a big, loopy straw hat. Lilah stooped down, picked up my bloodstained sundress off the floor, and tossed it on the bed behind us.

"If you soak this thing good, you can still get some wear out of it," she said as we headed out the door.

We took a cab to Delaware Brown's hotel. The Bel Air was about fifteen minutes away in a section of the city called New Kingston, where
the buildings were new and the Gaps, Benettons, and Guccis dotting
the clean, wide streets looked like they dropped down from a mall. The
hotel turned out to be a stacked monstrosity that was more upscale than
the Montego Bay. Each room had a tiny, narrow balcony attached to
it, just big enough for somebody to stick her nose out in the morning,
blink at the sun, and slip back under the sheets for another ten-minute
snore.

Lilah led me around to the back of the place like she knew where
she was going.

"There go Delaware's room." She pointed to a room on the second floor, about ten feet from the ground. The glass door that led to
the balcony was ajar, and long sheer curtains fluttered inside.

"Do you think he's there?"

She didn't answer but just stared up at the window as if she had
something on her mind, then abruptly turned and walked around to
the front. A group of college students, talking loud, slapping each

other five, and just getting home from wherever they'd been last night, piled through the door ahead of us and headed toward the elevator. Lilah joined in their laughter like she was part of the group. I followed behind, glad for my sunglasses and hat; there was no way in hell anybody who could see two feet in front of them was going to mistake me for a college kid. The two young receptionists at the desk, gossiping and giggling as they shuffled through stacks of paper, barely looked at the group as they nodded them past. We followed them on and then off the elevator, and then headed down the stairs to the second floor.

A young woman pushing a cleaning cart laden with old brooms, a dust mop, and variously shaped buckets and spray bottles glanced up at us indifferently as we walked toward Delaware's room. Lilah tossed her a sugary smile and the young woman returned it diffidently.

"Damn it! I left the damn thing unlocked," Lilah muttered when she tried Delaware's door and it didn't open.

"You didn't expect it to still be open, did you? Especially if he left. Did you tell him you were coming back?"

"Damn it!"

"Lilah, I've got to tell you something. I'm getting real bad vibes about this whole thing. Let's get out of here while the going is good. Maybe we can take our chances at the embassy. Level with them. Tell them the truth. I know a lawyer—"

"My husband, Sammy Lee Love, was stabbed to death, and I spent the night with the man who killed him, in case you've forgotten. Who the hell in the embassy is going to listen to what I have to say?"

She was on the money about that one.

She glanced back at the maid, who had turned into another room, and then reached down into her blouse, pulled out a couple of tens and straightened them out. "Wait here," she muttered as she headed toward the room that the maid had just entered.

They both came out a moment later, Lilah smiling sheepishly, shaking her head as if she was embarrassed about something, the young woman stuffing two of Lilah's tens into her pocket.

"I'd lose my head if it wasn't fastened on," Lilah said, like the stereotypical dumb tourist, and the young woman nodded in sympathy as she fumbled with a collection of keys. "I left that silly bag sitting right there on that couch. My husband left while I went to pick up my girlfriend." She nodded in my direction, and I rolled my eyes in disgust. "It's a good thing I realized it before I got down to that crafts market. Thank you, honey." Lilah grinned and gave the girl another bill after she unlocked Delaware's door. "Thank you so much."

"They're not supposed to do that, Lilah," I told her as the woman returned to the neighboring room. "That kid is probably going to lose her job when Delaware gets back and wants to know how somebody got into his room. She's bound to remember you, with you giving her so much money."

"That's why she'll forget me if it comes to that. Ain't nobody going to remember nothing."

"What about Delaware Brown?"

"What's he going to say? Somebody took some money that didn't belong to him? I'll be long gone by then."

"How can you be so sure?"

"About Delaware?"

"Yeah. About Delaware."

"Don't worry about it. I can handle him."

"Are you sure he's not there?"

"Yeah, I'm sure. Just come on in here, Tamara, before somebody else comes."

"Somebody else?"

"Ssshhh!" She shoved me in before her and closed the door, quickly locking it.

It was a generic suite. Save for the bright sun that peeked into the room through the fluttering curtains, we could have been standing in any embassy suites from Albany to Wilmington. There was nothing remotely Jamaican or Caribbean about it. But it was still larger than our place in the Montego Bay, and it made me wonder just who had really been calling the shots among the three of them.

A sliding glass door that looked like it needed a swipe with Windex was to the right. The couch, a dull brown corduroy in the middle of the room, looked like it had been pushed out of its place. Four very plump, overstuffed cushions were thrown on top of it with no thought to decor. A set of keys that appeared to belong to a rental car were on top of a small glass table to the side of the couch. A rug, an old Rya that looked as if it had been picked up at a warehouse sale at Sears, lay at a strange angle in the center of the room. The wide sliding doors of the closet to our left as we entered the room were open. Farther down the hall, I noticed, two other doors were closed—doors to the bathroom and bedroom, I assumed. The whole place had a funny, musty smell to it, like moldy bread and too many half-smoked cigarettes.

A pair of large, frayed sneakers were parked in front of the couch. I nudged Lilah and pointed toward them. "He's probably in there sleeping! And aren't those his car keys lying on that table?"

"No, he's not," she whispered back. "He told me last night that he wasn't driving that car no more because he was having some trouble steering. So he probably took a cab to wherever he was going the same way we did. What we doing whispering, anyway? The man ain't here," she continued, her voice low but close to its natural level. "I'm going to look around in here." She nodded toward the couch and the closet. "You want to start back there?"

"Why don't we both start back there. I don't want some pumped-up, hazel-eyed surprise popping out at me."

She shrugged her shoulders in a "suit yourself" gesture and led the way to the closest of the two closed doors down the hall. She stood in front of it for a moment as if waiting for something to happen and then opened it cautiously and glanced around inside.

"I told you wasn't nobody in here. It will go faster if we work separately."

I nodded toward the other door.

"That's the bathroom." Her eyes shifted quickly away from it, and we stepped into the bedroom.

"Let's get started."

"What exactly are we looking for?"

"That Kenya bag you were carrying on so about. And the money."

"What's all this money in?"

"I think it's in an envelope. A big yellow envelope like the kind they use in office buildings. There's nothing written on it though. It's just fat, fat and filled up and sealed with some tape. Real big bills," she said without looking at me. Her eyes got big as she described it, like a kid's do when he's making up a lie. I was beginning to have some serious doubts.

"Lilah, what kind of fool is going to keep that kind of money lying around? If there's as much money as all that, it's not here. There's probably a key to something, a safe deposit box somewhere, something in the airport, or one of the banks. There are plenty of international banks here. That would make—"

"No." She cut me off, her eyes wide, begging me to believe her. "I saw it, Tamara. I saw all that money. I know it's here. We just got to find it. Come on, help me look. Before he comes back." I must have looked doubtful, because she repeated, "I saw it, Tamara. I know it's here!"

"If I can just find my bag—I'm not even talking about the money anymore, Lilah, just my bag with my passport in it, and I'm out of here."

"Suit yourself. You'll be sorry when you see all that loot."

I have definitely lost my mind, I thought to myself as I leaned against the wall after she'd left the room, not wanting to sit down on the unmade bed, not sure where to begin looking first.

It was a small dark room, about half the size of the living room. I switched on the light, walked over to open the blinds, thought better of it and started going through the dresser, which seemed a logical place to start. I was self-conscious searching through the neatly folded underwear and shirts in the first two drawers—breaking and entering is not my style—but then I remembered why I was here, "helping a sister out," remembering the stake she said she'd put up for those two losers, and I realized I might as well do it up the best way I could. I ran my hand through his clothes and around and under the drawers looking for something, anything, taped to the inside of a drawer.

I was sure Lilah was mistaken about the envelope filled with money she'd insisted she saw. It was more likely that Delaware had put "all that loot" in a box or safe somewhere, like I'd told her. She may have seen it at some point, but I was sure it wasn't still hidden somewhere in the room. There was probably a key to something—a box somewhere or a hidden case—and I kept that in mind as I searched, opening several envelopes—one containing extra cash but not the kind Lilah was looking for, another a laundry ticket, and a third a bunch of receipts. I picked up and examined all the items on the top of the dresser: a set of keys that looked like they were to an apartment, assorted American and Jamaican coins, a wallet stuffed with American and Jamaican bills. Wherever he was he hadn't taken his money, and Delaware Brown didn't strike me as the kind of brother who would go anywhere without some cash. My suspicions were piqued again, and I glanced toward the living room, where Lilah was searching.

I looked under the bed, picking up several dust balls in the process, and pulled out a sandal, some blue briefs, and a pair of fancy red silk panties, which I assumed belonged to Lilah. That put the lie to her tale about not having made love to Delaware last night.

"Lilah," I yelled out almost in reflex, and then realized far be it from me, down here on my hands and knees in this killer's hotel room, to be judging the sister's character. Who knew what had really gone down last night? I had no business catching an attitude about the girl's sex life this late in the game, and a line from an old song Johnny used to sing about a pet snake who bit the lady who adopted him passed through my mind.

I knew (or thought I did) exactly who Lilah was before I'd gotten in that cab and come down here to look for that money. And it had been about the money, nothing else. About that thirty grand and where it could take my son. I pushed the underwear back where it was. But I knew one thing for sure: Lilah Love had left this brother's bed in a hurry.

I stood up, feeling my age, and glanced around the room to see what else I could find. I did a cursory search of Delaware's clothes hanging on the door and looked inside his shoes. I pulled out a large cheap black canvas bag, flipped it onto the bed and went through it, but there was nothing in the suitcase, either. Nothing.

I peeked out the door and called to Lilah to report my progress. When she didn't answer, I stepped outside the room, glanced down the hall, and then knocked on the closed bathroom door to see if she was in there. I knocked twice, then pushed the door open. It was then that I saw Delaware Brown's blood sliding across the floor from underneath his head toward my feet, a brownish red stain between the cracks of the chipped white and cream linoleum.

He lay midway between the toilet and the door, directly in front of the shower. A blue towel was knotted very loosely around his waist. His big arms were flung around his muscular chest like some overgrown baby raised in a gym. His hazel eyes were flat and stared at whatever he'd been looking at when life had been knocked out of him. He was dead, there was no doubt about that. His dark skin, once as pretty and smooth as a girl's, had that strange purplish, waxy luster that only death can bring. I flipped down the toilet seat and sank onto it, trying to control what I was feeling.

The wound was on the side of his head, his right temple, and he had bled around to the back. He had been struck either from behind or from the side with so much force he had probably been killed at once. He had fallen onto his back or been pushed onto it. Blood had congealed on the bludgeoned side of his face in a macabre pattern. I thought I might be sick, and I doubled over, fighting the nausea.

Jesus Christ! Lord help me! I cursed and prayed in the same breath as I got control of myself.

I got up off the toilet seat, stooped down and touched his arm softly with the back of my hand, brushing just lightly enough to tell if his body still held any warmth. He was as cold as the floor I knelt on. The stiffness of his body told me that rigor mortis had set in, and that he'd been dead at least four or five hours.

Could it be a natural death? A stroke? A heart attack? He could have passed out, fallen, and hit his head on the toilet seat on the way down.

But even as I played with that possibility, I knew it was foolish. The man was in better shape than me. I was whistling in the dark.

How had it been done?

I ran it through my head. He'd gotten up in the morning. Gone to the bathroom. Gotten in the shower—had he been killed before or after he showered? He had a towel around his waist. He'd probably been nude when he got out of bed. But if he had just showered, he might have thrown a towel around himself while he shaved, brushed his teeth, or just stood admiring himself in the mirror. Had he been shaving? I got up and looked for a razor but didn't find one.

Someone had surprised him. Someone had come up from behind him or from the side, hitting him fast and hard. It had to be someone strong, or maybe not so strong, just someone holding something heavy and hitting with enough force to put a hole in the side of his head. Had his killer come from behind the stiff, discolored shower curtain that concealed the tub? That would be impossible if he'd just gotten out of the shower. The killer had come from somewhere else. Maybe from the bedroom where she had just made love to him?

I pulled back from the horror of it, not able to catch my breath as the bitter taste of bile rose in the back of my throat.

And I thought about Lilah. Delilah Love.

"Goddamn you!" I couldn't bring myself to say her name, and I stepped away from his body, my heart pounding again, knowing now why Lilah Love hadn't answered when I'd called out before. She'd known he was dead as sure as she knew she could count on me to come back with her to help her get that money.

Was she still here? I wondered. *Waiting to knock the life out of me with whatever she'd used to kill him? Was that really why she had lured me back here? I was the only one left now who could connect her with these two dead men. How could I have been such a damned fool?*

I took a deep breath, wondering if Delaware had a razor stashed somewhere in the bathroom, anything to protect myself with if she came at me.

I'm not sure how long I sat there, stunned by what I'd found, not able to leave that room. Five, ten minutes—it was hard to tell. When the high, girlish voice came through the door I jumped, startled, my stomach in my throat.

"Hotel maid. All right to clean?" I wasn't able to get it together for a minute, and then finally realized who it was and what she wanted. *Should I leave? Stop? Stay? Scream?*

"Okay?" the voice continued, trying to ask for and receive permission with her question. "Okay if I come in?"

I made the muscles in my legs work, consciously demanding them to move, and stepped fast and lightly into the shower, pulling the curtain closed slowly without making a sound, dropping down into the tub, the grittiness cold against my arms and face.

I heard a door open and close and the loud, melodic singing of somebody with a lot of work to do who thinks she's alone. She was starting in the living room, and I listened as she worked, the tub damp against my skin, some water still in it. From Delaware's shower? It didn't matter at this point. I made myself focus on what the maid was doing and how long it would take her to get to the bathroom. Was she starting with the couch, the table? I heard her turn the vacuum cleaner on; she was doing the rug. She moved something, maybe the couch, and I listened to the sound of the broom as she swept the hall.

Was the bathroom next? She might stop in the bedroom. I heard her pushing the cart, first whistling and then singing a song loudly out of tune. She was coming here, skipping the bedroom, saving that for last. She probably did the same thing every day, the routine so familiar she could do it in her sleep. The living room. The rug. The bathroom. Starting with the sink, the toilet, the tub, the floor, fresh towels, new soap.

The tools of her craft banged in the wagon as she pushed it in front of her. I wondered how long it would take her to get to this door, and I felt sorry for her, this kid who had done nothing and would be haunted for the rest of her life by what she would find lying here on the bathroom floor.

She screamed twice, high-pitched and shrill, the way kids scream when they're kidding around or somebody yells who is scared for her life. I jumped even though I knew the scream was coming. I heard her running, crying as she ran, knocking into the cart. A bottle rolled. A broom fell on the floor.

I waited for a moment, counted to twenty, making sure she was out, and then I made my move, daintily stepping over Delaware Brown's body, heading for the living room. The car keys weren't on the coffee table where they'd been earlier, and the glass door that led to the balcony was opened wider than before. I followed Lilah Love's tracks out of the living room, onto the balcony, over the edge, and down about ten feet to the soft, green earth below.

8

I found two dollars in dimes and quarters buried in the lint and grit in the pockets of my jeans. I used the change to take a bus to within walking distance of the Montego Bay. When I got off I walked fast, avoiding people's eyes as if they could read what was on my mind by looking at me. I had nothing to worry about. With my head dropped down on my chest, my back stooped forward, and my sunglasses and the hat pulled low over my face, most folks gave me wide berth. I made it back to my room with no trouble and jammed the extra key into the lock, looking furtively from side to side before I entered.

The sigh that traveled from the bottom of my stomach to the top of my throat heaved out everything I was feeling—relief, distress, and simple exhaustion. I dropped down on the still-unmade bed, too tired to sleep and fearful of what closing my eyes might bring. I spotted the sundress that Lilah had picked up off the floor, and I stuffed it deep into the trash, trying to bury the memory of Lilah and everything else with it.

My room was silent and hot again, courtesy of the on-again, off-again air conditioner. I wasn't about to go out to the desk to complain, so I walked over to the window and managed to pry it open. The throbbing in my head started at the bottom my skull, making a beeline to my temples. I put my hands on either side of my head and squeezed, as if I could chase it away, but there was no relief. I tore off every bit of clothing I wore, searched through my suitcase again for some Advil, found the bottle and tossed down three without water, checked the door again to make sure I'd put on the chain, and slammed closed the window I'd just opened. I went through my suitcase looking for my Body Shop stuff, took out the dewberry bath oil and soap, which always calms me down. Then I went into the bathroom, locked the door, scrubbed out the tub with the hotel soap and one of my socks, plugged it with a washcloth, folded a towel in quarters and laid it against the back of the tub. I poured the bath oil into the tub and turned on the water full force until the scent of dewberry was all I could smell. I climbed in, sliding down until I was immersed in warm water and fragrance. Then I thought hard and long about everything that had happened to me and what I was going to do about it.

The only thing I knew for sure about the last twenty-four hours was that two men were dead, and they had both been connected by and to one young woman from Jersey City. What I didn't know was exactly what she had to do with their murders.

Could it all lie with Sammy Lee Love and the way he had died? One: One of the two of them had put a knife through the man's heart, and he or she knew they were going to do it before they stepped out of the car. They had to know it because they had to have the knife hidden on them. Two: He or she had to be strong enough to plunge that knife into Sammy Lee's heart. Despite what you see on TV, it's harder to kill a man instantly with a knife than it looks: you have to put it in just right. It's close, combat killing. Mano a mano. And it takes a stone-hard killer to kill somebody like that. Stagolee without the charm. Lilah claimed it was Delaware Brown.

The blade of the knife had been long and lethal, a switchblade that could fold up tightly into itself, small enough for a man to slide into a pants pocket or under a shirt with nobody the wiser. But it would have been hard to tuck it into a tight red tube dress, and Lilah's small pocketbook had been in my Kenya bag next to my knee.

I thought again about the seating arrangement last night, who had managed to sit next to whom. Sammy Lee had been first to the table, as was probably his style—the kind of man determined to get somewhere ahead of everybody else. Delaware Brown had sat next to him. I'd sat across from Sammy Lee, and Lilah had slid in next to me. It would have been nothing for Delaware, with those arms the size of country hams, to knock Sammy Lee hard against the wall and jab that blade into the proper place at the most opportune moment. The gunfire had sent me under the table by then, and everybody else was looking out for themselves. He knew he could count on Lilah to count her blessings and keep her mouth shut, since Sammy Lee had pushed her around a couple of hours before.

But Lilah could have put him up to it. Baiting him with a fatal mix of vulnerability and sex. She could be pretty convincing when she set her mind to be, I could testify to that. But I could be reasonably sure that Delaware Brown had actually done the deed.

But then who did Delaware Brown?

I settled back in my dewberry-scented bathwater and closed my eyes, allowing myself the luxury of imagining that I was anywhere but where I was. I sucked in my breath, counted slowly to fifty and exhaled, trying to release every bit of trouble in my soul. But I ended up right back where I started when I got into the tub.

But then who did Delaware Brown?

Lilah Love?

How much of what she'd told me was true?

She admitted she'd talked with Delaware about killing her husband and then when he'd actually done it, been surprised and devastated by what he'd done. Maybe that was the truth. Or maybe she'd had more to do with Sammy Lee's death than she dared admit. Maybe killing Delaware was the one way to be sure that nobody else would know just how much she had to do with it.

She'd readily admitted that whatever drug deal they were involved in was "about to get much much bigger." Drugs were definitely the devil's candy, soiling everything or everyone who had anything to do with them. Lilah had said that when she'd gone back to Delaware's hotel, he'd been agitated. They'd spent the night together—somebody had come by, she said, Delaware had gotten even more agitated, and then she "got out of there fast" after taking enough money out of his bag to pay for cabs and bribe that maid.

Who had come by?

She hadn't bothered to tell me that.

But she'd hadn't taken all Delaware's money. She'd left some in his wallet. Maybe she wasn't at heart a thief.

What had happened to make her hightail it out of Delaware's room so fast?

She could have killed him, waiting until he got up to go to the john before hitting him from behind. But then what did she need with me? Why not just stay in his hotel and look for "all that loot" she swore had to be there. Unless she was squeamish about hanging around a man who she'd just dealt with black widow style.

Unless something else frightened her.

Nothing bleeds like a head wound, and there had been enough blood dripping on that floor and around his body to tell me that whatever she or somebody had used to put a hole in Delaware's skull had been thick and heavy. Lilah was a small woman with tiny hands, tiny arms. Did she have the strength it took to kill a man as big as Delaware Brown?

Maybe there was a fourth player in this game, somebody teamed up with Delaware against Sammy Lee. Or maybe with Delilah against

Delaware Brown. Maybe Delilah Love had crossed her husband with her lover, then double-crossed her lover with somebody else.

Why didn't she tell me who had come by? She must have known him.

She hadn't been able to look me in the eye when she rushed through that part of her story. Maybe she'd been avoiding anything that could force her to tell more than she wanted to tell. I could kick myself for not pushing it more.

She knew the man who came by and she didn't want to tell me. But then why mention him at all?

Was she the victim or the victimizer?

There had been a subtle difference in the Lilah who I'd started the evening with—little-girl Lilah whining and bruised, with her Minolta around her neck—and the one who'd led me over to Delaware Brown's hotel room a couple of hours ago. That one had been tougher, surer, talking sweet and bribing that hotel maid to let us in the room without missing a beat. She knew her way around.

Was she capable of whatever it took to climb out of bed with a man she'd just made love to and brain him before he got his drawers on good?

Was she physically strong enough to do it?

I turned on the faucet with my big toe and a stream of hot water warmed up the bathwater, which had turned cooler than I like it. I settled back, my head resting on the folded towel, my mind running over my options.

Could I be in more danger than I wanted to admit? You never know when ole Mr. Grim Reaper, leaning on his scythe, will start whispering your name, talking so low you don't know he got you till you're in his grip. I'd seen it happen that fast—hell, I'd seen it happen that fast in the last twenty-four hours: Sammy Lee Love and Delaware Brown. They had no idea death would come looking for them like it had, on the arm of some just-out-of-school sister from Jersey City who liked to snap pictures of people she didn't know.

Was I about to fall prey to the same evil something that had taken them out? Those marks on Lilah's arms and the way the fear peaked in her eyes every time Sammy opened his mouth told me that in the realm of what goes around comes around, Sammy Lee was definitely in line for something that was coming around, and if Delaware put that knife through the man's chest, which it looked like was definitely the case, then Delaware Brown had something coming his way, too.

But what about me?

"Lord help me! What in the hell am I doing down here?" I screamed aloud in frustration. "Why can't I just have a normal vacation, take my free ticket and tired behind and relax in the sun like everybody else?"

I had to admit I'd gotten into this mess because of pure and simple greed. After Lilah had mentioned that thirty thousand, I hadn't heard anything else. What had she said earlier: *You know it's all about the money, you're smart enough to know that.* And it *had* been about the money, making enough for me to take care of my child, even if it meant taking a step into something that from the very first my sixth sense had told me to look at with one eye cocked.

Don't nothing grow from evil's bloom but evil's fruit.

I'd taken a mouthful of that fruit and was damn near choking on it. What was my next move?

I'd read something in one of the guidebooks about calling the embassy if you lost your passport, so I'd call them tomorrow. They would help me get out of this country as long as they didn't think I had anything to do with two dead fellow Americans, and there was no reason for them to think that. Yet. Thank God I'd worn the hat and sunglasses when I went over to Delaware Brown's. The cops knew about him by now, but there was no way they could connect me to him. Lilah, maybe, but not me. Every hour took me farther away from the scene of Sammy Lee Love's death. I hadn't told anyone what had happened, with the exception of Basil, and I knew he wouldn't rat on me.

Delaware Brown was dead, and Lilah was the only other person who knew I'd even been there. Nobody had come in to clean my room. When I got out of the tub, I'd take that sundress out of the trash and put it into the bottom of my suitcase. Maybe they would consider it personal property. Maybe they couldn't search it. Better still, I'd wrap it in a paper bag and drop it off somewhere, anywhere. Once I got rid of that dress, nobody would know anything I didn't want to tell them.

I would need money to buy a ticket back home and to maintain myself. At best, I'd probably be able to get out of Jamaica tomorrow afternoon or evening. I would just stay in my room until then. Not even look outside the door.

I'd stuffed five bucks in the sunglasses case that I'd put down somewhere in the room. I'd looked for it but hadn't found it in time to put in my bag before I'd gone out to the Stamp and Go. It had to be in my room. But I needed more than five dollars, and there was only one place I could get it with no questions asked. My best friend, Annie. She could wire me what I needed. Jamal was staying with her so I could talk to him, too. A weary smile formed on my lips when I thought about my son. It would be good to hear his voice.

And then, for no reason at all, I thought about that time I'd almost made love to Basil Dupre on my kitchen floor back in Jersey. That was one day when two of my strongest instincts had definitely been at war—responsible mother versus horny hussy—and as the tenderness and heat of his lips grazed and lingered on my throat, a reckless sweep of desire had nearly shaken me inside out. But not quite.

It would have been some good lovin'.

I leaned my head back against the makeshift headrest and gave the hot water faucet a hard nudge with my toe.

The real Jamaica? You should have asked a real Jamaican.

But there was nothing I could do about that now.

The room was pleasantly cool when I left the bathroom; the air conditioner had seen fit to come on again. I got the dress out of the trash can, wrapped it in some newspaper and then in a bag I'd gotten from the crafts market. I'd drop it outside somewhere as soon as I got a chance. I sank down on the bed, and closed my eyes. If I tried very hard I could pretend that my life was back to normal, that maybe I'd just finished soaking and was in my tiny little bedroom back home lying on my bed in my bright yellow room and thinking about nothing. Maybe I'd go fix myself a cup of Sleepytime tea, flip on the tube and watch the eleven o'clock news. Jamal would peek in at some point; we'd talk about school for a while — how he was doing, what he wanted to do — and then we'd say our good-nights and I'd read a little before I drifted off to sleep. If I tried hard enough, I could pretend that I'd never heard of Delilah Love or Sammy Lee or Delaware Brown and that the possibility of whatever was going to be could still be between me and Basil Dupre.

It was going on nine when I called Annie collect, the only way to call the States from the Montego Bay.

"Oh, girl, I envy you. Down there in that hot sun getting all black and pretty," she said after I'd finished apologizing for the collect call. She laughed the deep-bellied laugh that always brought a smile to my face. "I know you're having the time of your life."

"You could definitely say that."

"What you going to bring me back?"

Me.

"I need a favor, Annie."

"You always need a favor."

"I need you to wire me about four hundred bucks." I'd given them the imprint of my MasterCard when I'd checked in, so I didn't think I would have to worry about paying the hotel bill, at least not for the present. Four hundred dollars would cover my one-way fare back home, and give me about fifty extra dollars for food and any other minor expenses.

I could almost see her mouth drop open as they formed the words.

"Four hundred dollars! Damn, girl, that's a lot of money! Tamara, what's wrong? What's going on?"

I could hear worry in her voice and the panic that rides on the end of somebody's words when they truly care whether you live or die. I cared about her too much to tell her the truth, because there wasn't a damn thing she could do about it anyway. I'd gotten myself into this mess, and I had to get myself out.

"Nothing. I just need some extra money."

"Extra money! Something must be wrong, with you calling from Kingston, Jamaica, needing me to send you four hundred dollars."

"I misplaced my pocketbook. You know that Kenya bag I carry? I think I left it on a blanket at the beach and somebody walked off with it." It was just dumb enough to sound convincing. I didn't bother mentioning the loss of my passport—that would really send her to Nut City.

"Left it at the beach? How did you manage to leave your pocketbook on a blanket at the beach? Tamara, that doesn't sound like you. Have you gotten down there and lost your sense? Must be some man down there somewhere. You must have met somebody. Don't be letting anybody take your money. Don't be falling for no lines from any of them smooth-talking, pretty brothers down there. Left your pocketbook on a blanket at the beach? Be careful down there with all that sun. Just 'cause you're black don't mean the sun can't bake your mind."

"Annie, I feel stupid enough as it is, please don't make me feel any worse. I just need the money without a lecture. Please." I was definitely telling the truth about feeling stupid.

Pause. "Are you sure you're okay?"

"Yeah. Is William in town?" I hoped she wouldn't share my misadventure with her husband. He was a good brother, but he liked to tease. He'd be on my case about it for the next two decades.

"No, he took off for Chicago yesterday afternoon. He'll be back sometime Friday. Don't worry, I'll keep this to myself. Thanks for

Jamal though, he's been a lot of company and help. Mama has been having some problem with her pressure, and I've been on the phone fussing with her fool of a doctor about her medication. Jamal's been keeping me sane. Listen, I can probably pick up that money at an ATM on the way to get her medicine tomorrow morning. I don't think I can get that kind of cash on my credit card, but don't worry. I'll wire it from the Western Union in the Pathmark during lunch. You won't have any trouble picking it up?"

"Wherever it is, I'll get it. Thanks, Annie, you know I owe you. Is Mama okay?" I wondered if that note of worry in her voice was coming from another reason. She hesitated before she answered.

"Yeah. I think she'll be fine. How about you, Tamara, are you sure things are okay?"

I reassured her again, trying to take some of the desperation out of my voice, and she put Jamal on the line.

"Hey, Ma. How things going?" Just hearing his voice, how normal it sounded, made me feel better, and suddenly a feeling of well-being swept me and I knew that everything was going to be okay. It wasn't hard for me to pretend that I was okay too. Jamal could always tell when I lied to him, and I was relieved that I didn't have to.

"Fine, son. I'm fine. Are you being good?"

"No, Ma. No, I'm not being good. Yo, Ma, what do you expect me to say? I'm not a kid anymore. I know how to behave when you're not around."

We both laughed then, me realizing just how foolish my question must have sounded.

"I wish you were down here with me, son." I meant it from the bottom of my heart. If he'd been here, I'd never have been sidetracked by Lilah Love. That's one thing kids are good for—they keep you walking the straight and narrow.

"Yeah, me too, Ma. Next time, okay?"

"Yeah, sweetheart. Next time." There must have been a catch in my voice when I said it, a note of finality or desperation, and I could tell by the dead quiet on the end of the line and the anxious tone of his voice when he spoke again that he'd picked it up.

"Ma, are you okay?"

"Fine, son. Just a little tired."

"Talk to you later?" There was a hint of worry in his voice still, so I made my voice sound strong, confident.

"Sure, baby. I'll call you first thing tomorrow night. I might be coming home a little earlier though. I miss you."

"You miss me that much? To be coming home early?" He didn't sound convinced.

"More than you'll ever know. Let me talk to Annie."

"I love you, Ma."

"I love you too."

He yelled out for Annie, and she got back on still scolding about the dangers of good-looking men, cheap rum, and too much sun, the worry still in her voice as she begged for more reassurance. She finally took me at my word when I told her I'd had a vacation she wouldn't believe and that I was tired as hell but basically I was fine and I'd be staying here in the hotel room for a day at the most, where she could reach me if she needed to, and I'd be on an Air Jamaica flight probably tomorrow night after I got the money.

I was so convincing I actually believed it myself.

9

Hunger was crawling around the pit of my stomach when I finally woke up. It was late, nearly eleven. I had slept as long and hard as if I'd been drugged. The phone rang six times before I got myself together enough to answer it, and then the line went dead. I assumed it was Annie, and picked it up quickly when it rang again. I was right, it was Annie, but this was the first time she'd called.

She was calling from work and sounded distracted and tense. Would it be all right, she asked, if she sent the money later than she'd planned? She'd had to go in early because of an emergency, and she hadn't been able to get to an ATM. She'd probably be able to get the money and send it later on this afternoon. I assured her it would be fine. What else do you say to a sister who will send you that kind of money no grief given or questions asked? I tried to put a devil-may-care lilt in my voice to hide my disappointment.

After she hung up, I watched the noon sun stream in through the window for a minute, turned the TV on, then off with the remote control, and lay back wondering who had made that first call. I finally called the front desk, but all they could tell me was that the call had come from outside the hotel.

There were only two possibilities: Basil Dupre and Lilah Love. You don't talk bad about a man's dead mama and expect to hear from him again, so that left Lilah.

I'd assumed that the embassy in Kingston would operate like the Department of Motor Vehicles back in Jersey. Bureaucracies are usually the same everywhere. I expected to be put on hold, given to the wrong person, asked for irrelevant facts, then put back on hold again. I was pleasantly surprised. I immediately talked to somebody who sounded like she knew what she was talking about. She asked me how my passport had been stolen, and I explained how I'd lost it at the crafts market (a little spin on the song and dance I'd handed Annie). Passport theft was on the rise, she explained sympathetically, advised me to report the theft to the local police (which I told her I'd do, praying she wouldn't check up on me), and asked me to come to the embassy. The whole thing, she assured me, shouldn't take more than an hour or two if that, since they could call the States to check my Social Security number and other vital information to verify my citizenship. If all went well, I could be home by tomorrow night.

I didn't mention the fact that I didn't have any money. The more I told them about my situation, the more they'd want to know. If they got me a temporary passport, that would be all I needed from them. After I'd finished with the embassy, I called the front desk and asked for the location of the nearest Western Union office.

Hunger started gnawing at me again, so I searched for my sunglasses case with that five dollars, found it behind the dresser, and grinned like I'd just hit the Pick 6. I had enough now to get a bowl of that conch soup I'd shamelessly wolfed down at lunch my first day here, some bread, which was free, and a cup or two of coffee. I didn't want to risk putting anything else on my room bill. I'd be up the creek if they asked to see my card for some reason. When I picked up Annie's money later on tonight, I'd eat a decent meal. Pig out. Binge. Reward myself with every bit of Jamaican food I'd been missing. I slipped into my jeans, a T-shirt, and sandals, tucked the extra key into my pocket, and headed out, hunger giving me the strength to face the world.

I walked the two flights down, wondering if I should go back for my sunglasses and hat, and then reminding myself that there was no reason to go incognito—nobody was going to connect me with anything that had happened. Nobody but me *knew* what had happened. But there was a strange tension in the lobby when I stepped off the elevator. I could sense that something was up. People seemed to be avoiding each other's eyes, and the smiles of the women at the front desk looked brittle enough to break.

Or was I imagining it?

I headed for the small restaurant off the lobby, sat down at the first available table, and ordered a bowl of soup. I saw and heard nothing as I slurped it down, aware only of its hot, peppery taste as it slid down my throat. As I scraped my spoon over the bottom of the bowl when I'd finished, I glanced up and noticed a very tanned woman with blond hair smiling at me from the next table. She looked like she wanted to talk, which I didn't, so I grabbed a *Gleaner* that somebody had left in the seat of the chair of the table next to me and absentmindedly leafed through it.

The beaming faces of Jamaican children in neat school uniforms carrying bookbags smiled at me from a photo captioned "Faces of Our Children." An article about a thirteen-year-old describing how he wanted to become a pastor reminded me of how little about this country I'd bothered to see. What a fool I'd been to think that I could see the "real" Jamaica with losers like the three I'd hooked up with. I felt ashamed of myself. Here I was, an African-American coming into a country like this where nearly everyone looked like me, believing without a second thought the worst about it. I was as bad as some fool tourist stopping over in Harlem or Newark and assuming some jackleg hustler with a toothpick in his mouth and his cap on backward was going to show her "real" black Americans.

The real Jamaica was in the beaming faces of the children in the pictures in front of me. It was in the scent and spirit of the Caribbean Sea that touched nearly everything on the island, and in the flowers that grew with such wild, colorful abandon. Here was Jamaica, full of people like those I knew back home, folks loving and learning and raising their kids with no money in the best way they could. God, I'd been a jackass. This whole sordid mess had served me just about right. I jammed a wedge of bread into my mouth in self-disgust and was about to turn to the back of the paper, when a headline at the bottom of page 2 caught my eye.

NO PROGRESS IN KILLING OF TWO

Up to press time last night, no progress has been made in the killing of two unidentified patrons of the Stamp and Go, a notorious bar in West Kingston.

The bread stuck in a thick, yeasty lump at the top of my throat.

The two men were the victims of foul play early Tuesday morning.

I took a long fast, sip of coffee.

According to Victor Spaulding, the proprietor of the establishment, one of the victims had been seen there on at least one other occasion. Police speculate that one or both may have been involved in illegal activities. One or both may have been citizens of the United States. The killings are thought to be connected.

I folded the newspaper in half, and again, compulsively, into quarters and pushed it to the other side of the table like I could catch something from it.

The soup in my stomach began to curdle. I felt a sweat break out under my arms. I knew who one of the men was, but what about the other? Who was he?

"Well, are we safe?"

The voice and the question it asked caught me off guard, startling me, as if somebody had just read my mind, and for a moment I couldn't connect anything or put the voice where it belonged. Then I realized it had come from the woman at the next table, the blonde with the deep tan. I looked up, a dazed expression on my face. She gave me a slightly condescending smile. "I'm sorry, I thought you were American." She turned back to her plate.

"I am."

"Then hello!" she said cheerfully in a voice aged by too many Marlboros. The thin warm hand she extended was lightly covered with freckles or liver spots, I wasn't sure which. "I'm Hannah Grant, from Bridgeport, Connecticut." She glanced around, and then lifted a copy of the same newspaper I'd been reading from a straw bag that told me she'd spent some time in the crafts market too. "I was reading about those tourists earlier. Do you think it's safe here, with them killing tourists and all? I assume they were tourists since one was American. But the other was German, I've been told."

"German? But it said . . ."

"German, my dear. German," she repeated, with a certainty that said she knew what she was talking about.

My mind raced back to that night and who had been standing at the bar. There had been a German there. The one with the black duffel bag. What connection did he have to all this?

If Hannah Grant noticed the distress in my face, she didn't show it; she rambled on pleasantly. "We had a driver, a nice enough fellow, who told us what happened. I think he wanted to scare us so we'd hire him full-time. He doesn't know that the States aren't like they used to be. It takes more than a couple of murders and everyday violence to scare us Americans these days. We've gotten use to it. Small potatoes.

"Anyway, the cabdriver, I think his name was Patterson—that was what he had on the front of his car anyway—told us that one was American, black American, and the other was German. I didn't ask him how he knew. I really didn't want to know, if you know what I mean. They're not telling the papers anything because they don't want to scare us away. Do you think we're safe?"

Despite what she said, I understood now. She was a slightly scared tourist looking for reassurance from a countrywoman. I played the game.

"We're probably safer down here than a couple of cities I can name back home," I joked, on automatic wit. She laughed a good-natured cackle.

"Of course, you're right. I'm Hannah Grant, from Bridgeport, Connecticut. But I said that already, didn't I? That's a sign that you're getting old, repeating yourself like that. Do you mind if I join you?"

"Sure." I wanted to know more about the German tourist she'd mentioned. She moved over to the table, picked up the paper and quickly put it back down.

"So you saw this too, huh? I was reading it earlier. I always read the local paper when I go to a foreign country." She folded the paper back into quarters like I'd had it and replaced it. "I'm traveling with my husband. He's elderly, older than me anyway, and not doing too well. This is supposed to be a second honeymoon. We never had a first. Kids came too soon."

She spoke quickly, moving her head a quarter of an inch with each word, and her short hair, which I realized now was actually silver rather than blond, bounced with each word. She looked directly into my eyes, as if she had nothing to hide and assumed that I didn't either, and I realized suddenly that she reminded me of Mrs. Morse, my favorite English teacher in high school. She had given me a copy of *Their Eyes Were Watching God*, the first love story about black people I'd ever read.

"I'm Tamara Hayle," I introduced myself. Those eyes seemed to expect it.

"Tamara. That's such a pretty name. My granddaughter is named Tamara. You must have a sweet nature. It's funny what names can tell you about a person. My husband's name is Hugh, Hugh Grant, like that handsome young actor who got caught with his hand in the cookie jar—or something else in the coochie jar, might be more accurate." Her eyes sparkled in amusement as she giggled mischievously. I was pleasantly surprised by her bawdy sense of humor. "In his case, though, my husband's, he had that name long before that young man was born, but whenever he says it, 'Hugh Grant,' people look disoriented for a moment, like he's lying.

"He's upstairs waiting for his bowels to move. We're heading to the other side of the island—Ocho Rios—after he comes down. It's a little more pleasant there. More tourists. It's a pretty enough country though, isn't it?"

I nodded, trying to figure out how to gracefully steer the conversation back to the cabdriver and the German. Finally, I just asked her.

"So what exactly did that driver say?"

"About what was in the paper?"

"You said it was a German who was killed?"

She looked at me like she didn't understand me, and then patted my hand as if to reassure me. "Don't worry about it, dear. It happened in a part of the city where they tell tourists not to go. There are always those parts to an island, especially one as poor as this one. Naturally there will be those parts, think of our own country. You shouldn't worry about it."

"I'm just curious," I hoped that was how I actually sounded.

"Well, he said, Patterson the driver said he was killed, him and another man. You know what he said, though, and it scared the bejesus out of me, the way he said it, I mean." She leaned forward, as if sharing a secret. "He said that the German had been killed with 'great brutality.' And then he described precisely how."

"What did he say?"

"Well, he said that word had it that somebody had slammed the man's nose bone straight through to his brain. That must have been one hell of a punch, right? To shove that man's nose through to the back of his head. Isn't that horrible to say it that way? Straight through to his brain. They didn't put *that* in the papers, did they?" she added with a knowing grin and an exaggerated shiver. "They don't want to scare away the tourists. Besides bauxite, it's the biggest industry down here, you know, tourism."

"What about the other one?"

"The other what?"

"The other man who was killed. The paper said there were two. Did he say how the other one died?"

I knew, of course, how Sammy Lee had died, but that hadn't been mentioned in the newspaper either. I wanted to know how accurate the cabbie's information was. But even as I asked it, I knew the driver probably had the real deal. Kingston, like Newark, was one of those places where folks who like to talk about other people's business basically get it straight, with a little tint around the edges to give it some color.

"I think he said he was stabbed. Right straight through the ticker. It must have been like something out of *Pulp Fiction*. Did you see that movie? God! The language! They must have said the *f*-word at least a dozen times!

"It must have been a gang. A gang of thieves and murderers! Who would think such a pretty country with so much sun would have people like that living in it? You halfway expect something like that in places where the sun never shines. People getting depressed and doing bad things and whatnot, but not here. Yet on the other hand, look at California, you've got plenty of sun shining there and all kinds of awful things happen. You're not from California, are you?"

I told her that I wasn't.

"Thank God. I wouldn't want to offend. I guess there are reasons why they tell you not to go to certain areas."

I didn't say anything. I just stared at the coffee that was left in the bottom of my cup.

"Are you okay? Don't tell me I've upset you. As long as you stay out of the places they advise you not to go, you'll be fine. Get yourself one of these handsome young drivers to drive you around. They'll keep you out of trouble and take you safe places, and if you're lucky, even not-so-safe places if you know what I mean," she added with a wink.

She looked up then and waved to somebody across the room. "My husband Hugh. He just got off the elevator. I guess his bowels finally moved. Well, it's off to Ocho Rios for us! Much nicer place, you don't see so many poor there. We're staying at a nicer place there. All-inclusive. You can't be too careful when you're on a fixed income. Get as much as you can for free. You okay, my dear?"

I shook my head that I was, not willing to trust my voice.

"Well, I'm off. Good to talk to you. Good luck to you," she said over her shoulder, slipping out of my life as breezily as she'd slipped into it.

I sat there for a moment, watching her and her husband leave, not sure where to put this new information.

The killings weren't connected. How could they be? I knew who had killed Sammy Lee Love. Delaware Brown had killed Sammy Lee Love.

I made my way out of the restaurant, barely noticing who was in front of or behind me.

I'll be safe soon.

I held on to that thought, repeating it like a prayer.

I'll be safe.

I stopped by the front desk, picked up another paper, decided against reading it, and put it back down. I asked if I'd gotten any calls, hoping against hope that maybe Annie had been able to send the money earlier after all, but nothing had come in. The young woman at the desk was the same one who had been on the night I'd gone out with Lilah and Sammy. She avoided my eyes, not looking at me when I spoke to her, as if she was afraid of me.

What did she know?

But then in the next moment, I was sure that I had imagined it.

Calm down, I told myself. *Get it together.* Nobody could connect me with anything. Lilah maybe, but not me. I tried to remember the name of that beach where Basil had taken me.

I walked to the elevator and pushed the up button. *They knew about Delaware Brown by now, but there was no way to tie me to him.*

The two men were dressed in cheap gray suits, rumpled and too warm for the heat. They approached the elevator, and I stepped back, letting them get in front of me. Everything about them, the low, unhurried tone of their voices, their eyes lingering on and probing each item upon which they rested, told me they were cops.

"This is connected to that other matter, I'll wager that, but what we could have learned is cold by now." The tall one spoke in a low, clipped voice, as if he was talking to himself. The other, shorter, nodded his head deferentially, respectfully, telling me who was boss.

"After you, miss." He was young, with big, shy eyes. A rookie. Polite. I managed a smile, my heart in my throat.

What if they were heading to my room? Did they know which room I was in, even though they didn't know what I looked like?

I thought about the dress in my room. I had an impulse to turn tail and run, up the two flights back to my room, but it was too late.

I avoided the tall one's eyes, and my face grew hot, making me feel guilty even though I hadn't done squat. I studied the numbers on the elevator, watching it like it was going to start talking as the young one pressed the third-floor button.

"Going up, ma'am?" I nodded and exhaled, not even realizing I'd been holding my breath. At least they weren't heading to my room. But just as quickly the relief disappeared.

Lilah was on the third floor. Room 314. Had they finally identified Sammy Lee Love? Had they connected her to the murders in the Stamp and Go? Or to Delaware Brown?

If she'd actually come back to her room, she wasn't above implicating me to save her own skin, that was one thing I knew for sure.

"What do you think we will find, sir?" The younger one had forgotten my presence or assumed I wasn't a threat. His voice was high, a boy's voice. Deferential, like mine had been when I was a rookie. But the older cop, using his right as a commanding officer to ignore his subordinate, chose to do it.

The elevator creaked to the third floor and I got off with them, my head dropped low, wondering if Lilah would dare to lie to my face if she saw me behind them, and in the next minute wondering how I could slip down the stairs and back to the safety of my room. I followed dumbly behind them, too scared to risk drawing attention to myself.

Was it Lilah who had called this morning? If she was there, what would she tell them about me?

I ran through my options, what I would say if they confronted me. Thank God, I'd put through that call to the embassy and reported my passport missing—maybe I could fall back on that.

There was a cop in uniform standing before us as we approached the door. He seemed to have come from nowhere, his face empty of expression, his arms stiff like he was keeping a vigil. The young one stopped abruptly and turned toward me, barring me from going farther. But the door was open, and I could see in a single glance the savagery they had tried to hide.

The curtains had been torn from the rods and hung in tatters down either side of the window. Glass from a broken window sparkled on the floor. An ugly crack like a spider's web split the mirror that faced us, and the contents of the top drawer—lacy red panties, bikini swimming suits, bras and slips—were tossed in a mass of lace and color on the floor. Curse words—"fuck," "shit," "cunt," and others that made no sense and had poured from a madman's mind in a language I didn't understand—were smeared in black blood or excrement on the walls and door and mirror. A tight red dress, Lilah's tight red dress, lay like spilled blood in a dirty pile on the floor.

"Dead?"

I couldn't hear my own voice; I didn't know I could find it. But the look they exchanged told me I had uttered that one word aloud, and their eyes shifted back to each other and then away from mine. The young cop stepped inside the room and slammed the door in my face without answering.

10

Raythell Broom.

It was years since I'd heard that name or seen that face—the turned-up nose and elfin smirk that made him look like a sly, blond version of Michael Jackson. His eyes were as round and brown as a fawn's, and as empty as if he'd been born without a soul. But you wouldn't notice it if you brushed against him getting on a bus or standing in line at the grocery store. You wouldn't know that evil had touched you. Evil has an ordinariness to it, yet when it touches you it lingers like the smell of spoiled fish.

My grandma would cross herself when she was in "evil's presence," as she put it. It tickled the hell out of me and Johnny to see her do it. She wasn't Catholic, had never been Catholic, didn't even know anybody who was Catholic. We weren't even sure if she did it right, that graceful thin finger traveling up and down, to the right and to the left of her head and heart. She did it faithfully though, like the old folks rub their grandbabies with prayer oil or spit over their shoulder to chase away demons.

It was a chilly spring morning near Easter Sunday the day my path crossed Raythell Broom's. Pink and blue Easter bunnies were sitting in mounds of cellophane grass in baskets in store windows, and most of that morning the only thing that was on my mind was what I was going to cook for Easter dinner: lamb or turkey, sweet potatoes or potato salad, collard greens or green beans. That all changed quick.

Raythell Broom walked into the delicatessen on Manor Street, and shot to death everybody who was in it: the small Polish woman with the funny snaggle-tooth grin who owned it, her big-eyed baby boy, her father from the old country, and six customers, running late for work sipping their coffee at the worn Formica counter. It was the randomness of it that got me; that you could walk into your death at the hands of something like Raythell Broom, that the man who stood behind you could take away all you were or could ever be.

I was one of the first cops on the scene, me and a red-haired guy named McDermitt who up until that day had only given me grief, always tossing out the stupid remark or shitty joke meant to get under my skin. He never said the words — "nigger," "bitch," "cunt," "spade" — but he thought them, felt them, and made sure I knew it. But what passed between us that morning united us, told us that we had something sacred that was missing from Raythell Broom. He wiped that color/gender bullshit right out from under both of us, and we'd stood close enough to touch that morning, trying hard to hide our feelings, overwhelmed by the horror and stillness that was in that room. I still hear from McDermitt every now and then.

When we came to get him, Raythell Broom was standing at the counter like he was getting ready to pay for the jelly doughnut he was munching, his AK-47 leaning against the counter next to his knee like a cane. Verses from the Bible — from Judges, the Second Book of Samuel, Deuteronomy — were scrawled on the wall in somebody's blood, as if he was mocking God.

The words on Lilah's wall brought it back — the crooked capital A's, T's crossed with precision, tiny circles used like dots, a glimpse into a madman's heart. My fear of what had happened to Lilah told me what my eyes hadn't been allowed to see—that someone as evil, as crazy as Raythell Broom had been in that room with her, and the fear and dread I'd felt when I laid eyes on him all came back. I had the answer to that question I'd asked myself yesterday, why she had dragged me with her across town to look for the money at Delaware Brown's: She had been afraid.

I'm not sure how long I sat on the bed once I got back to my room, running things through my mind, posing questions to myself that had no answers. The spirit had been kicked out of me. I felt a lingering sense of grief for Lilah, but also guilt-laden relief that things had come to closure, that the string connecting me to the three of them was cut. Lilah was the link, and now that link was broken.

Or was it?

I couldn't get her out of my mind, even though I owed her nothing. I knew that she had used me and would have done it again if she'd gotten the chance. God only knew how much truth there was in anything she'd told me about her life. Yet even though I'd known her for less than three days, I knew that for the rest of my life she would pop into my dreams and sneak into my thoughts, bringing back what I needed to forget when I least needed to remember it. Delilah Love. It was her vulnerability that had touched me. I had seen myself when I looked at her—my own youth, sadness, and foolishness—a Tamara Hayle long gone except for her slow-healing wounds and memories.

When I finally looked at the clock, I knew it was too late to get to the embassy. I didn't have the strength to walk, and even if I'd felt like going, I didn't have the money to take a cab. I'd have to put everything off until tomorrow morning or whenever I got the money from Annie.

I wondered if she had called or left a message, so I called the front desk. There were two messages. Both had come in while I was down at lunch; neither was from Annie.

The first, from the hotel manager of all people, requested that I stop by with additional identification for verification of my MasterCard, which was the last thing I needed to hear. Either the cops or the girl at the desk might have mentioned something about my possible connection to Lilah that had cast a shadow over my presence. Whatever it was, they probably didn't have enough on me to make a stink about it, not yet anyway.

The second message was a telephone number without a name, and a request for me to call at once. There was no answer when I dialed it, and I wondered if this could be the same caller I'd missed earlier. I'd left my name and number with the woman at the embassy in case she needed it. The number wasn't familiar, but it was probably her.

On impulse I called Annie, collect again, not even sure she would be home. I needed to hear her voice—something familiar that I could grab onto. I was just about to hang up when she finally answered, her voice distant and tense. "Hello." She sounded tired, but she perked up when she knew it was me.

"Tam, it's good to hear your voice, girl."

"You know that consulting job I took on, they really put me through it today, girl. All kinds of shit."

It can't be nothing like I'm going through down here, I thought but didn't say.

"I just walked in the door. I had to take Mama to the hospital. I've got to go back."

I knew from the tone of her voice, which had risen about an octave, that a four-hundred-dollar loan to me down here "funnin' and sunnin'" in the islands was the last thing on her mind.

"You just happened to catch me here. I been on my feet all day long. Mama started feeling dizzy when I went over there this morning. I got her some more medication, but that made me late. They were all over my ass. You know when anything goes wrong, it's always the colored lady's fault. Bitching about nothing. I didn't even get any lunch, and when I got home, Mama was feeling worse, so I took her to the hospital. I came back here to check on Jamal and make sure he got in okay, and then I went back. The Western Union at the Pathmark was closed, and I only got half the money you needed, that check I put in last week didn't clear, so—"

"Annie, you're making me tired just hearing you girl, take it easy," I said.

She paused. "Yeah. I'm trying to."

"Take a deep breath, Annie. Count to ten."

I heard her take in and blow out her breath.

"Do *not* worry about me," I said. "Don't worry. Don't! Don't worry about the money. Take care of your mother."

She sighed hard and long before she continued. "But Tamara, I promised you."

"No, you didn't."

"I may not have said it, promised it, but I said I would. I'm sorry I let you down. First thing tomorrow morning. I'm going in late, so I'll be able to do—"

"Do it when you get a chance, Annie."

"Are you sure you're okay?"

I owed her the truth, and I almost gave it to her, then reminded myself in the next breath that even if she had the energy and time, there wasn't a damn thing she could do about any of it. What could she do? Call the embassy? The Jamaican police? They were just looking for somebody to pin something on. What could I say to them that wouldn't get me in deeper? My prints were still on the knife that had killed Sammy Lee Love if they decided to look. Better to take my chances on my own, and not bother my friend with more than she could handle.

"Get it to me when you can, Annie. Don't worry about it. Just kiss your mother and tell her I'm saying a prayer." Annie had her hands full. I'd just have to stay put until she could find the time to get the money to me. If I didn't have it by tomorrow afternoon, I'd have to consider other options, and I'd have to ask somebody else to put the bill on their credit card, if it came to that, which hopefully it wouldn't.

I'd probably end up calling Jake. I'd have to psych myself up to the embarrassment of asking him for money, especially in a situation like this. Since he's a lawyer, I couldn't get away with the bullshit excuse I'd handed Annie. He'd know a lie when he heard it, especially coming from me. He'd ask questions, I could count on that, and he'd expect some answers. He'd work them out of me, if it came to that, which would present an altogether new set of problems.

Maybe I could throw myself on the mercy of the hotel manager. Maybe I could use DeLorca, my ex-boss and the chief of the police department in Belvington Heights—the town near Newark where I used to work—as a reference, maybe he would vouch for me. Maybe the embassy had a travelers loan fund.

I turned on the TV for noise and for lack of anything else to do and started to pack, wondering what my next move should be, if I should call Annie back and tell her not to bother or call Jake or my sister Pet, who is always as broke as me. I opened my suitcase, tossed some clothes in, and then took out my frustration on the Frommer's guidebook to Jamaica that lay on the night table next to the bed. I threw it as hard as I could at the opposite wall. It hit a picture, a cheap print of Dunn's River Falls, and the frame tipped precariously. I picked up the book and carefully straightened the frame; being charged for wrecking the room would be all I needed. When the phone rang again, I picked it up without thinking, assuming that Annie was calling me to tell me something she'd forgotten.

"Tamara?"

The voice stopped me short. It was a man's voice, high and squeaky, one that I knew I had heard before. The accent was American, and sounded familiar—New York? The Bronx? Not Newark, I was sure of that. He said my name like he knew me.

"Yes."

"Did you get my message?"

My back stiffened, and my stomach got tight. I wasn't sure why.

"Are you alone?"

Was it the embassy? I wondered. Or the police? No, they would sound Jamaican. They wouldn't want to know if I was alone.

"I met you at the bar. The Stamp and Go. That place in West Kingston. The night your friend got stabbed," he continued, not bothered by my silence, as if he could read my mind. I froze, my hand tight on the receiver, my heart pounding. My voice was tight and hurt coming out.

"Who is this?"

"Lacey. A friend of Delaware Brown's."

I remembered him now, standing against the bar when we entered, the man Delaware Brown had gone to meet, with the voice that sounded like a kid's and those eyes like Delaware's. What had been in those eyes as hazel and secretive as Delaware's? What had they been hiding?

Don't I know you from somewhere, man? You been around somewhere I been.

Sammy Lee had said that to him, and I'd sensed from the way he said it that it had been more than Jersey City. Had it been the joint? Something to do with the "business" that was getting bigger?

"I don't know you. I have nothing to say to you."

"You saw what happened to Delaware Brown, didn't you? You know what happened to my brother, don't you? You still got nothing to say to me?"

I sat down on the bed, bending the cover on the Frommer's guidebook back and forth like some kind of fool, then dropped it down on top of my clothes in the suitcase. His voice had deepened when he said it. Was he threatening, taunting me? I thought about Raythell Broom.

"How do you know about that?" I knew about it because I'd been there, and he must have been there too. I realized after I'd said it that

I should have kept it to myself, that it told him more about what I knew than I wanted him to know.

"You were there too, weren't you? Don't try to bullshit me. Not the real-deal motherfucker here. You can't bullshit the bullshitter," he said, his voice turning nasty, higher-pitched and testy.

"What do you want?"

"You know what the fuck I want."

"We have nothing to talk about."

"You don't really believe that, do you? I know you ain't telling me that shit!"

"Say it now, what you've got to say, and make it quick."

He paused. "I want my money. I want my fucking money."

"What are you talking about?"

"I want my money that you got from that bag that little whore you hang with took. The money I left with Delaware Brown."

"I don't know—"

"Don't be telling me 'I don't know' now. You ain't going to be fooling me. I know about you and your girlfriend, baby, and one of you bitches has got my cash."

"Delilah Love?" I asked, not quite getting it, and then suddenly understanding in a flash of horror that he was Delaware's friend, the man in the bar who knew him, who Delaware had told where he stayed.

A place called the Bel Air, like that old car I used to drive, man. Room 207 . . . same as the number my mama hit when she took us to the shore that time.

"That little whore who was sitting up there beside Delaware when it was happening, she know how things went down." He laughed then, the way a man laughs when he thinks nasty things about a woman, and it hit me in my gut, as deeply as anything else he'd said. "Where did she put it? I know the game you two bitches are playing."

"You know what you did to her!" My voice choked when I said it, and I hated myself for my weakness.

He had to be the fourth player in this game of death they'd dealt me, and he'd been playing all the time. He was thin, but maybe he was stronger than he looked, strong enough to knock somebody's nose through to his brain. Strong enough to kill a man with something hard and big to the back of the head.

He'd known where Delaware Brown was staying and how to find him. And Lilah. If she hadn't seen him, and she probably had, he knew she was there. He could have followed her from Delaware Brown's easy enough. Or Delaware could have told him, bragging about this cute young piece of ass that was his whenever he wanted it. Or maybe he had known her all along. Maybe he had double-crossed her in the end too.

I screamed into the phone then, half crying, cursing at the top of my voice and letting loose everything I'd felt for the last two days on this disembodied voice with its Jersey accent on the other end of the line.

"You killed her, didn't you! For nothing but money. You killed her! Why write that kind of shit on the wall about her? Why would you do that, you crazy motherfucker? And now me? Forget it, you lousy, murdering bastard. I know what you are. I know who you are! Just stay the fuck away from me."

"I don't know what you're talking about. I just want my goddamn money. I just want my goddamn money," he chanted like a demented kid.

"I don't have your money!"

"You ain't fooling nobody. You're mixed up in this shit good, Tamara Hayle. You're mixed up in it good."

"How do you know my last name?"

Silence. "I asked you how you knew my last name." I screamed louder, and his voice was harsh when he replied.

"I know everything I need to know about you. I know where to find you. I know how to wring your nasty, dirty little neck for it if I need to.

You have it for me when I come over there, you hear me? You better find it before I get over there."

I slammed the receiver down hard into its cradle, shutting out that voice.

Somebody came by . . . and Delaware got agitated and mad all over again, and I got out of there fast . . . and came back here.

Lilah had known there was some money, and gone back for it because greed will get you every time—it almost got me. It had, as she said, always been about the money. And it still was.

Whatever money Lacey was talking about, he thought I had it. Who else would have it but me? Where else could it be but with me?

He had seen me with the three of them. Met me with them at the Stamp and Go. Maybe they had even told him that I was working with them. If he'd looked in her room—and he'd obviously looked—and didn't find it, then he would come looking for me. Had he tried to force her to tell him? If she had the money, why hadn't she just gone on and given it to him? Had she hidden it somewhere that she couldn't get to?

When would he come for me?

Did he really think I was stupid enough to be waiting for him to come and get me? To even talk to him again? He'd called me for another reason, but what could it be? Where could this money he was talking about be?

Every instinct I had for survival kicked in now, as I searched for the second time in two days for something to defend myself with. There'd been nothing then and there was nothing now. Nothing so I could meet him on his own terms. I'd need a gun for that.

But I knew one goddamn thing for sure. He wasn't going to take me out the way he had taken out the others, smacking the life out of me, then scrawling some shit on the wall as my epitaph.

Like Raythell Broom.

The phone rang. I watched it, not taking my eyes off it, willing it to stop as it rang five, six, seven times.

But what could he do to me in here? Why was I so afraid?

I reached for it finally, picking it up as warily as if it would burn me.

"What do you want?" I screamed out the words, hating myself for trembling.

"Tamara?" The puzzled voice was familiar and deep, and touched me to my roots. "Tamara. It's Basil. What I want is for us not to part as we did. Will you come with me for a drink?"

11

"Why didn't you call me?"

"I'm not the kind of woman who expects men to come to my rescue."

"Pride will be your downfall, Tamara Hayle. You have to bend in life or it will break you." He said it like a sage bestowing a bit of wisdom, but then he smiled a smile that curved his sensual lips, and told me that he wasn't altogether serious. "I could tell the moment you walked across that lobby that you were afraid. You have very truthful eyes, Tamara, even when your lips are dishonest. Your eyes never lie."

We were sitting at a tiny table on the terrace of a small, elegant restaurant off Waterloo Road in New Kingston. We'd had that drink Basil had requested and followed it with a light dinner. The night was cooler than the day had been. It had rained earlier and the air was misty, dampening the stiff table linens and delicate purple flowers that spilled onto the terrace from a nearby bush. Everything had a slightly gauzy glow to it, which could have been either the effect of the rain or the sweet, smooth Tia Maria that slipped down my throat.

We'd hardly spoken when he picked me up in the lobby of the Montego Bay, and our first half hour together had been tense, filled with mutual discomfort; neither of us apologized or mentioned what had happened before. When we finally began to talk, the weather was our main topic of conversation, which should tell you just how cautious we were being. But when he asked me what had happened since we'd seen each other last, it all poured out. I was surprised by how much better the unburdening made me feel.

He said very little as I spoke, but listened intently, occasionally asking me to clarify some point or fill in details that I'd left out. When I finished, he leaned back in his chair, his arms loosely crossed in front of him, and his eyes probed mine as if searching for some secret.

"So you think he killed this woman, the pretty one in the tight red dress, and now he is after you, this man who calls himself Lacey."

"That's the way it looks to me."

His eyes sparked with anger when he said Lacey's name, bringing back for a moment the Basil Dupre I knew, the one with the reckless, sinister edge who my brother Johnny would have warned me against had he known him, even though Johnny had that edge himself. His knee touched mine cautiously under the table with a soft nudge that sent a thrill fluttering through me. I shifted away, embarrassed by my vulnerability, and then finally let my leg settle back against his, amazed by what his touch did to me, even as slight and seemingly accidental as it was.

"Is he Jamaican?"

"American."

"He threatens women, so he is a coward and a bully. He lives in Kingston?"

"I don't know, but I don't think so. You're not thinking about getting involved in this mess, are you?" The speed with which he asked his questions hinted that his interest was about more than just dinner conversation.

He shrugged, took a sip of his Tia Maria and smiled at me over the rim of his glass. "I didn't say that."

"You don't have to. I know you."

"Don't be so sure of what you know."

I didn't challenge him, but I knew I understood more about him than he thought I did. He lived by a code of honor, revenge, and violence, one that as a cop I had been trained to despise, but that I also respected, as only someone who has fought against it can. I knew he was tough, and would fearlessly protect himself or someone he loved and believed was threatened, despite any obstacles or consequences that were hurled his way—definitely not the kind of brother who would end up dying in bed. I had to admit I was glad he was on my side.

He rose, nodding for us to go into the restaurant, when the mist turned to drizzle, and we settled at a table near a large open window just in time to miss a downpour. "It's the beginning of the rainy season. Showers come and go like this. It makes everything fresh and new. You can almost smell it," he said, inhaling the air as if he loved its fragrance.

The air did seem fresher, and I could smell the sweet wet scent of flowers and grass growing somewhere in the darkness. Or maybe I'd just been stuck in that damn room in the Montego Bay so long, inhaling air hot with my own nervous sweat, that everything smelled better. It was Wednesday night, and I hadn't thought about or felt anything but fear since Monday.

The rain had dampened Basil's thin white shirt and, nearly transparent, it stuck to his skin with each gesture, emphasizing the taut, powerful muscles of his arms and shoulders. But he had the slender, graceful hands of an artist. He reached across the table and gently ran his fingers along my palm and between my thumb and fingers, and I pulled my hand away, dropping my face down to hide what I was sure was a blush. Up until that moment, I'd had no idea my fingers were an erogenous zone.

"You should have called me," he chastised me again, hinting this time at more than just my need for his protection.

But I wasn't sure if I was ready to put aside my anger over his life and the doubt that shaded my feelings about him, even though those doubts seemed small in comparison now to what I'd been through in the last few days. I've never been one of those women who feel safer when they're with a man. Even in my twenties, hitched to my fool of an ex-husband, I always slept, as they say, with one eye cocked. I've always taken care of myself with a blend of toughness, mother wit, and plain dumb luck, and I'm proud of my resilience. But I'd stumbled into a world of killers that was foreign to me. I had no idea what it took to survive. It was a world that Basil understood, and since I'd been here with him, my fear and dread had settled far back in my mind. I didn't know if that was a good or a bad thing, letting a man I didn't completely trust have so much power over my sense of security, but this was the best I'd felt since I'd come down here. I took another sip of Tia Maria and decided that, at least for now, I'd let the chips fall where they might.

"Should we begin from where we left it?" he asked, as if he could hear my lingering doubts and internal conversation; he'd always had a second sense about me.

"And where was that?"

"How you were feeling before you decided that I was a dishonorable man."

"But I was just repeating what you'd said about yourself."

"But you meant it."

"Yes, I did. Because you told me what you did about the, quote unquote, death of your sister?" It sounded preachy, but I said it anyway, my grandma's moral sense rearing its head.

"Why is it so important to you?"

I hesitated for a moment, not sure if I wanted to go into my general unwillingness to trust men too quickly or completely. But then I realized I had nothing to lose by telling the truth. "I don't like lies or liars."

"Lies, like the truth, always have a reason."

"The truth is the truth."

"Truth is as you see it, nothing is as easy as it seems," he said after a moment. "You'll excuse me for saying this, Tamara, but things come so easily for women like you. American women like you."

"Black women. Not just American. African-American," I quickly corrected. "There's a difference."

"More American than you think."

"Well, I'm not going to get into a cultural thing with you," I said, suddenly annoyed. "Just what are you trying to say?"

He chuckled with some amusement. "Don't be angry." He gently touched my arm, soothing me. "It isn't about that at all, though one difference I must admit is that more of us disbelieved the lies the white man told us about ourselves. But what I'm saying, Tamara, is that there are assumptions Americans make about life and what it owes them. The luxuries that you have—yes, even black Americans—come so easily for you and so hard for those of us in countries like mine, even though we own our countries. We and the World Bank," he added with a wry smile that took some of the bite out of what he'd said before.

"What does any of this have to do with your lying about your sister?"

"Only that you wouldn't have been so quick to condemn me as a liar, to take for granted that everything in the world comes down to good and evil, lies and truth, if you understood more about me. Everything is so easy for you. You have never seen what I and many who have grown up like me have seen. You live such soft lives, Tamara. Where truth and goodness and right and wrong are easily and quickly defined. They are a luxury for me. My life so often turns on gut survival; morality is never an absolute." He started straight ahead, and his voice was bitter.

"You take so much of the good life for granted. Always air conditioners to chill the air. Always enough good food to eat and strong spirits to drink. Always ice to cool your Cokes. You live assured that life is there for your pleasure. My world is much harsher."

"You know very little about my life or me," I said irritably, but I'd cringed when he said "air conditioner." I was glad I hadn't fussed to him about the one in the Montego Bay.

"You sound pretty sanctimonious for one who is so unsure of the truth," I said finally.

"What makes lies and a liar is different in our worlds, Tamara. I don't know if we can ever bridge that difference."

"Basil, lies are lies. Truth is truth. Good is good. Evil is evil."

"You are a seeker of justice, Tamara. You like to know that good will always win and evil will always be punished. But I've seen too much gray to believe in black and white or that justice is anything but a word. I've seen evil come out the victor more often than not."

"So just what do you believe in, Basil?"

He looked puzzled for a moment. "Believe in? What do you mean?"

"What do you believe in? God? Truth? The devil?"

He paused as if he was pondering what to say. "What I feel. What I love."

"And what is that?"

"It varies according to the day of the week and where I've spent the night," he said solemnly, but there was a gleam of laughter in his eyes, telling me he didn't want to be taken seriously. "You don't believe me, do you?"

"I don't know what to believe about you. Or if I should believe anything about you at all."

"What are we to do, Tamara? About the feelings we have for each other?"

"Well, I don't—"

"Don't try to deny it. You know what I'm talking about. You've known from the first moment we saw each other, Tamara. That first time I kissed you in your new husband's home. And what will it come to?"

"I honestly don't know."

"We live our lives by different standards, with different rules."

"Yes," I agreed, sounding sadder than I meant to. "Yes, we do."

There were differences between us, and I was old and wise enough to understand that in the end they would probably destroy any bridge we'd managed to build. Should I cross that bridge when I came to it?

"There are absolutes for you, Tamara. There are none for me. You're a cop. Me? Well, I don't have to tell you who I am," he added with a smile. "I'm not ashamed of it or what I've had to do to get by. Yet I don't want things between us to end badly, and I'm not sure what that means. I don't usually have these feelings about women." He looked genuinely perplexed. "It's amazing to me."

"To me, too."

"But I'm sorry," he said finally, his eyes growing dark, and softer. "I'm sorry if I hurt you with that thing about my sister. The lie that wasn't one."

"It's hard for me to trust, Basil. I've been hurt so often it's hard for me, and when I'm lied to it destroys everything I feel or could ever feel." Those words surprised me when I admitted them. I'd always guarded that particular truth about myself, but it was the truth of who I was and why I so often found it difficult to get involved with suitable men whom I knew I could love. I couldn't think of another person, with the exception maybe of Annie after too many drinks, whom I'd admitted it to.

"I honestly don't know if you should trust me, Tamara," he said quietly. "I know the grief I'm capable of inflicting. I'm not sure if I want that responsibility."

"I don't know if I want to give it to you."

"But you have been on the edge of my life for longer than I care to remember. I am haunted by what could be between us."

I took a quick sip of my drink, unwilling to let him see what I knew was in my eyes.

"Do you want to start again where we left off?" I asked. "About why you lied to me. About what you were trying to share about your life and your sister Bettina? I promise I won't take off down the beach."

"There's no beach to run down."

"So I have to listen."

He smiled but then turned serious. "When a family is as poor as mine, your honor is all you have. You would have to come from what I come from to understand how I could call her dead, but she was to me."

He glanced out the window and then back at me as he spoke with deep sadness.

"My country has changed since I was a boy. It is harder, its simplicity gone. Drugs and politics have become a blood sport. And yet there is still a sweetness to this place, a joy that I can find nowhere else on earth. I leave. I return. I leave, I return. Like to a woman who has gotten under my skin." He smiled a sly smile that let me know who that woman was. "I always carry it with me in my soul, and I forgive it and love it as deeply as my own flesh."

"Why did you leave?"

"Lives here are narrowed by things you can't control. By class, violence, loyalty. If you are born to suffering, then you suffer like your father did.

"I left to change our lot. Make life better for those behind me. I've made and lost and made again more money than my father ever dreamed of. I brought Bettina to the States—but you know the rest. It shames me to think of what she became. I don't need to go into that again."

"Where is she now?"

"Here, in Jamaica for now. After she left Newark, after her 'death.' " He turned to me with another smile, acknowledging what had gone between us before. "She lived in London, took up with Scratch, that guy I told you about, and then others, but usually him. She's home now, came to bury my mother. But not for long."

"In your mother's place in West Kingston?"

"Up on the hill." He nodded toward the shadow of the Blue Mountains which I could see in the distance. "It's beautiful there, like paradise. It belongs to my brother Noel. I stay in it when I come home. I took my mother up there hoping the peace would heal her."

"Your brother? I thought you said you just had sisters?" I didn't disguise the doubt that was clearly in my voice. I tensed up, preparing myself for some new lie. He chuckled but not maliciously.

"I say he's my brother, Tamara. But he's not really. Blood brother, Tamara. Like brothers. Blood but not the same blood. We were boys together, came to manhood together. He's richer than most of us now. He booked reggae and dance hall acts back when it was still handled by black men. Used our culture to make himself big money."

"And where is he now?"

"London."

"So you were near the Stamp and Go to see about this Scratch, your sister's boyfriend?" I asked, remembering what he'd told me earlier when we were at the beach.

"I don't approve of him."

He reminded me so much of Johnny suddenly I grinned, puzzling him with my reaction. It was that big-brother protectiveness, disapproving of anyone and anything.

"You sound like my brother used to sound," I explained, remembering how Johnny and I would fight about my boyfriends.

"But you are not like my sister," he said quickly. "My mother used to warn me about my devotion to her. Don't fatten roaches to feed to fowl, she used to tell me. Bettina would never be worth my effort. My mother said that until the day she died."

It was a hell of an ugly thing for a mother to say about her child, but he'd said it without rancor, so I didn't comment on it. The last thing I needed was to make another off-color crack about his mama. My relationship with my mother had been a hurtful one, and I suddenly felt sorry for this protected younger sister with her strong brother and a mother who would compare her to chicken who didn't deserve fat roaches. No wonder the girl had gone wrong.

"She sounds like she's got spirit," I said in her defense.

"That's one way to put it."

"Weren't you talking about forgiving folks a couple of minutes ago?"

He smiled, but said nothing.

"Can I meet her?"

"Bettina?" He shrugged, with something I couldn't quite interpret in his eyes. I was curious about the girl now. But then I thought better of it. I still had to get out of this country while the getting was good. "Maybe another time," I added quickly. "Next time I'm down here or next time she's in the States."

"I assume then that you're cutting your time down here short?"

"Yeah." I wasn't up to sharing my tale of woe about the details of waiting for Annie's money. He guessed my predicament despite my reticence.

"Did you ever find your bag?"

"No."

"What are you using for money?"

"I'm getting along."

"Tamara?" He said my name softly, with a question in it.

"A friend is sending me some money from the States."

"So when is your friend sending it?"

"Tomorrow. Sometime tomorrow."

"And you're leaving after that?"

"Probably."

"And tonight, after you leave me?"

"Sneaking back into the hotel," I said, without thinking of the implications.

"Sneaking?"

"A little problem with the bill."

He shook his head, chiding me, and I felt like a naughty kid for a moment longer than I wanted to feel it. "Don't scold me," I said, and meant it.

"How much of a problem?"

"Whatever it is, Basil, it's not your problem. They have an imprint of a credit card, but now, all of a sudden, they might want some more identification, which, of course, I don't have."

"So the police have been sniffing around, and they probably know you're involved somehow with this bad business, but they don't want to risk insulting a tourist with no hard evidence, but they do want to make sure you're who you say you are and that you can pay your bill."

"That's the way I figure it too."

"I'll call Mavis and see what she's heard."

"After what I said about your mother, she'll probably believe the worst she's heard about me. She may have even contributed to the tale."

"She's a good churchgoing girl like the rest of the women in my family, save the little one. She won't think the worst of you or smear your reputation."

"As soon as I hear from my friend Annie, and get verification from the embassy, I'll be on my way back home."

"Tomorrow?"

"Tomorrow night."

"And the other thing. This man who called you. Lacey?"

I didn't answer for a moment. It was amazing how thoroughly I'd managed to push him from my mind. Then the face, the voice, and the fear I'd felt came slamming back, but I responded with bravado. "What about him? When I'm back in the States I'll be back in my own territory. I can take care of myself back there. I'm sure of that."

"But you're not back there yet."

"I'm fine, Basil. I'll be fine," I said with conviction, meaning to discourage any more discussion, and he took my hint.

We sat quietly for a few moments, both of us listening to the soft sounds of the night—the chirp of insects in some green corner and the rain as it hit the roof and sidewalk. I glanced out the window at a small boy walking in the rain with his mother. She held a shopping bag in one hand, and her son's hand with the other, bending to talk to him as he jumped over puddles. He was skinny with a baby's face, but the large solemn eyes that caught mine were the eyes of an old man—old souls, my grandma used to call kids with eyes like that. Johnny had been an old soul in his way; so was my son Jamal.

How different were our worlds, Basil's and mine, and how much did it really matter?

"I've heard some things that bother me," Basil said quietly, bringing my attention back to him. His eyes were those of an old soul, I decided, deep and sad.

"I told you before where I grew up, and I still have ties there. One of those kids, the ones who did the shooting, is the son of a friend of mine. His daddy is dead, his mama trying to keep things straight. She's not as strong as you—her son needs a father's hand, which I've not been able to offer as often as I should. He's not a bad boy, this one, but trouble likes him.

"He came home the other night, his mother says, full of his own manhood and rich with American dollars. She got it from him that someone had paid him, he wouldn't say who, to shoot up that place, the Stamp and Go. So it was as I thought."

"The shooting was a distraction?"

"To call attention from the killing that was done."

"Two men died that night. Neither was shot. Who was the intended victim? Sammy Lee Love or the German?"

"Or both."

"But what was their connection?"

"Maybe nothing, or maybe they were tied in ways we still don't know. Maybe that connection is closer to you than you think."

My face must have told him what I was feeling.

"Why don't you come with me, up into the mountains where I'm staying? I have to come back to the city early tomorrow morning with my sister, and I can get a car then, and bring you back tomorrow afternoon. You can rest in the mountains until then. It will do you good to get out of Kingston. Come with me?"

His eyes, which had changed so much that night, from angry to tender to sad, searched mine now for an answer. I'd known it the moment he touched me.

He paid the bill, and slipped his hands into mine and led me to the door. But then he stopped suddenly and turned to face me.

"You asked me earlier what I believe in. I believe in me, Tamara, and in you, and how good we will be together."

12

And we would be good together.

The ride into the Blue Mountains was straight up, the road so crooked and steep that whenever I got the courage to open my eyes and glance down, I quickly closed them again; the ground seemed to plunge abruptly down on either side. I'd gotten used to the wild beauty of the island, but there was a special mystery to it at night: the shadows of sugarcane hovering ominously on the edge of the road; the pure, sweet fragrance of the flowers when I least expected it; and from somewhere far, the musty smell of the sea.

The roads were bad, the paving worn and potholed, but Basil drove with an expert's skill, taking the curves evenly and never losing speed or control. The higher we climbed, the farther away the blaring sounds fell, and so did the heat of the city. The night lay before us as black as sable, the stars and moon hidden by the overcast sky. The thin yellow streak of light from the motorbike's headlight cut bravely through the darkness, illuminating only what lay ahead, and there was no sound save the motor's hum. It was as if the rest of the island had dropped off the edge of the world.

I leaned into his back, jostled by the bike and holding on to him tightly, both for dear life and the simple pleasure of feeling his body against mine. We rode for nearly an hour before he pulled over to the side, stopped briefly before what looked like a private road that was in far worse shape than the one we'd just left, and shifted into a lower gear to climb it.

The road had become mud in several places, and the bike swerved dangerously as we plowed through it. We finally pulled up in front of a large structure that looked pale gray in the dim moonlight and was lit on the outside by security spotlights, which accentuated its austere plainness and the flowering vegetation that grew in bursts and clumps.

The house was made of aging white stucco and looked like the kind you see in old movies about Hollywood—like an old-fashioned Spanish hacienda or mission house. I could smell the delicate fragrance of orchids and the heady scent of allspice floating in from the grounds that surrounded it. The shadows of ferns and bougainvillea dangled from trees and the iron fence. It was as if I'd stumbled into some exotic, magical garden.

The front door was made of dark wood and graced with an elaborate metal knocker in the shape of a flying fish, and squeaked loudly as Basil pushed it open. We stepped into a spacious foyer with floors of heavy brown Mexican tile and high ceilings dotted with wooden fans. The room was cut in two by a polished wood staircase that led to rooms at the top. The ceilings and walls of the rooms I could see were elaborately trimmed in the same dark wood—mahogany, I assumed, which I'd read was native to the island—but the darkness of the wood was softened by the paleness of the stucco walls and the pastel blues and yellows of the cushions in the furniture.

I followed Basil out to the terrace, which was dark and encircled the house. The lights that he'd turned on were dim, and the large hurricane lamp that he brought out to the terrace threw off little light. All around, as far as I could see, was darkness, and but for the chirp of crickets and tree frogs singing in a chorus, there was silence. Far down the mountain, the lights of Kingston shimmered like a crystal necklace strung across the sky.

"You don't see the struggle and despair, how the sufferers suffer, as they say it, from up here," Basil said quietly. "But I can never allow myself the luxury of forgetting just how few people live like this, in a place like this one."

I glanced back inside for a moment, struck again by everything— from the shine on the mahogany trim to the braided jute rugs to the carved wooden vases waiting to be filled with flowers. When he'd called it paradise, he hadn't exaggerated. I wondered about Noel, the man who owned this place, and about the money it took to maintain it.

The lights in the living room dimmed, flickered for a moment, and then went out completely, leaving us in darkness before they twinkled back on.

"He has his own generator with a mind of its own that goes on and off according to its whim," explained Basil as he left to attend to it. He rejoined me on the terrace after a moment with another hurricane lamp and an old boom box that ran on batteries. He dropped a pile of tapes into my lap, and I sorted through them.

There was mostly reggae, ska, some dance hall—Peter Tosh, Bunny Wailer, Judy Mowatt, Marcia Griffiths, and some old things that had been out for a while in the States. I handed him the sound track from *Dead Presidents*, a film that Jamal had taken me to see on Mother's Day. Basil put it on, and then went into the house and came back with a bottle of Wray and Nephew rum and some sodas.

"No ice," he said apologetically.

I was still feeling the effects of the Tia Maria, so he opened a Ting for me. I quickly gulped down the sweet, grapefruit-tasting soda, and the bubbles tickled my nose.

"So you are here by yourself," I said, wondering about his sister and conscious suddenly of the silence and emptiness of the place.

"She may show up later," he said. "The place is big, and she comes and goes as she pleases. She's probably with that man I told you about earlier. She knows I don't want him here while I am. He'll drop her off, come back when I'm gone."

"The guy you mentioned before?"

"Scratch."

"They grew up together?"

"You might say that."

"What do you mean?" There was something in the tone of his voice that piqued my curiosity.

"Whores together."

I was startled by his harshness, and I knew it showed on my face.

"The truth is the truth," he said ironically, but he'd noticed my response, and he explained further, his eyes avoiding mine, his voice distant. "You find yourself in dire circumstances when you're young, no resources except the body God gave you. You find that there are women—very rich foreign women—who will pay for something you would do for free." He shrugged then, slightly defensively, as if expecting my disapproval.

"But then that past will haunt you because you thought you had the power, but they had it, and you have paid with your soul and with what is most sacred within you. It takes years to get back what you allowed to be stolen." He shifted his eyes from mine, and I wondered if he was talking about some part of his own youth, when he had been that poor and desperate. His eyes told me nothing. But then again they did. He never revealed more than he intended.

"But it is different for him, for Scratch," he continued. "He used to hustle women, but he's gone on to bigger things now. More lucrative and evil than selling a stroke of the big bamboo to rich tourist women for whatever he can steal. He's not like so many of the others. He has no soul to lose."

"And your sister?"

"She has no idea who she is dealing with. Despite what she thinks they have in common, there is still an innocence about her."

I doubted if he knew his sister as well as he thought he did, and I was beginning to understand the anger that he felt for her. I thought I understood now the underlying source of that lie about his sister's death: by making her "dead" when he spoke about her, he had killed that part of himself. I wondered if there were parts of his youth that had shamed him, and that added to his shame of her. But I sensed it was best to leave it alone.

"They met again in London. After she left the States. They were part of the same world. The drugs. The whoring."

"This was all after she died . . . in your mind?" I asked, cautiously.

"After she died in my mind," he repeated, with a touch of defiance.

"But you said his brother owns this place?"

"He does." He took a sip of his Coke.

"And you tell him, Scratch, he can't come by, even when your sister has invited him?"

"It's complicated."

"Tell me."

"I told you."

"Tell me again."

"We're like brothers, I told you that. Noel and me. But don't ask me about his family. Or mine for that matter."

I let it rest for a minute, and then started up again. "It takes big money to take care of a place like this," I said neutrally.

"Yeah."

"You said he was in London?"

"Yeah."

"But he stays here when he's in Jamaica?"

Basil laughed. "Tamara, I feel like I am on trial. You can't leave it behind you, can you?"

"What?"

"The cop. Asking questions like a cop."

"Does it bother you?"

"Of course it bothers me. I don't like cops."

"I don't like them either some of the time. But what are you trying to say?"

"You tell me." But then he smiled again, letting me know he was teasing, and then quickly answered as if he'd chosen to ignore what he'd said before. "He rents it to rich Americans and Brits. Most people who live here could only dream of a place like this. I could only dream of a place like this," he added with a self-deprecating chuckle.

"But doesn't Scratch have as much right, more right to this place than you?"

"There's bad blood between them now. I'm not sure what happened in London, but Noel wants him nowhere near him now nor what belongs to him. It's one of the reasons he has asked me stay here when I can, especially when Scratch is in town, to keep an eye on the house for him, to make sure his brother comes nowhere near it. They're blood but he knows Scratch is no good."

"But blood is blood." I was thinking of my own connections to my family, dwindling as it was, and Basil's to his—to his wayward sister and his dead mother.

"And bad blood is bad blood," Basil answered philosophically.

"But a younger brother?"

Even though I hadn't met either of them, I was beginning to understand the tie that bound Bettina and Scratch. It was the anger of their family. "But you've forgiven your sister."

"But Bettina is not Scratch. Everything Noel does is legitimate now, he wants no dirt left under his nails."

"And Scratch is dirt under his nails."

"That's one way of putting it."

"So he wasn't always legit, your friend Noel?"

"He's in London. Leave it alone, woman, let the man be!"

"I'm just curious."

"You know what they say about curiosity, Tamara."

"Killed the cat."

"You said it, not me."

"Now what am I supposed to make of that?"

He shrugged and laughed. "The less said about all of these matters, the better, Tamara. Don't question so much."

"That's who I am, Basil. I question. Maybe it's my way of understanding you, of learning to trust you," I added.

He paused for a moment, as if he was thinking about it, and then he explained. "Noel is like me. Doing what he has to do to get by. He did what he did, it paid off handsomely, and now nobody asks any questions. Scratch is a reminder of things he doesn't want to remember. A younger brother who reminds him of the evil in himself. But let's not speak of that now. Let it go, my love. Let it go."

Maybe he was right. There was a timelessness to this night, and I settled back to savor it. What did I need to know of this place and who owned it except it was an added reward to the last few hours? My time with him had made up for the craziness of the last few days. I deserved this, I decided, all of it, no questions asked. I deserved the luxury, the serenity, the peace. It was as if God had finally decided to smile on me, as if nothing—not the violence, the fears, or the squeaky threat of Lacey—could touch me. I felt truly safe for the first time since I'd left home.

I sat back, sipping my Ting, listening to the tape and squelching the cop part of me. And when the familiar opening chimes of "I Miss You" and the throaty voice of Harold Melvin floated from the CD player, I allowed the mix of memories that takes me over when I hear that song to have their way. I thought about the summer nights and sensual slow dancing of my fifteenth year—and of my mother's death and my first love, Randy, one of the "bad boys" Johnny gave me so much grief about.

I thought about the fervent, secretive rub of his young hard body against mine, of that July of necking, petting, doing everything we could until I'd finally "surrendered," giving myself to him on a rainy afternoon in his tiny room off the kitchen of his house on South Orange Avenue. This was one of those songs, our songs, the Dells, Aretha, Barry White—every damn song that played that summer seemed to turn on every hormone I had. I'd lost my mother and my virginity the same summer. All of it came back now, making me wince with the memory of its sorrow and pleasure.

It was as if Basil could sense where my mind had gone when we began to dance, my body blending into his as if he were taking all the sadness of those memories from me. Dancing is a sexual pantomime, telling you how a man will move when he is inside you, how rhythmic, how tender he will be. And as Basil held me close, guiding me into him with each movement, I was lost in the sensual rhythm of his body. His lips touched and then parted mine with a gentle insistence that grew stronger, and I responded to the urgency they demanded.

There aren't a lot of men who know how to kiss, and I've had my share of losers. There were the tongue thrusters of my youth, those brothers who amazingly, even into their thirties and forties, still seemed to believe that the way to ignite a woman's passion was to open their mouths as wide as they could and thrust their tongues halfway down her throat. I could count on my left hand the men in my life who actually knew how to kiss, and on my right those whom I'd actually enjoyed kissing.

When he kissed me now, running his tongue lightly over the soft inner edges of my lips, tasting them, demanding more and then lingering on my throat, my chin, I was aroused so suddenly and with such intensity I felt dizzy for a moment. We pulled apart then, and sat back down on the couch, barely touching, saying nothing.

"Come with me," he whispered after a moment, his breath touching and tickling the inside of my ear. Blindly, I followed him up the stairway into his bedroom on the far side of the hall.

It was a simple room, mostly white, which made it seem at once cool and strangely chaste. The bed was large and high off the ground, and there were four big pillows piled at the head that looked soft as if they were made of goose feathers. There were small night tables on either side of the bed, both made of the same heavy wood as the headboard, and a circular, elaborately braided straw rug at the foot. We sank into the bed's voluptuous softness as we sat down. His closeness made my heart race.

"I can make you no promises about where it will go from here or even what we will mean to each other in the end," he said quietly.

"I don't remember asking you for any." Promises were the last thing on my mind.

"As long as you understand that."

"I understand it. Are you sure you do?"

He smiled then, acknowledging that his risk was as great as mine. The truth of the matter was that promises, commitment, the other tender traps that we're supposed to ponder and reflect upon before we jump into bed with a man, were irrelevant to me at this point. I'd left that particular illusion right beside my wedding vows to my exhusband. I'm wise enough to know that words are as easy to forget as they are to say. All I knew was a simple truth: I had wanted him for as long as I had known him.

He kissed my lips, gently at first, and then with a hunger that took my breath away. His lips traveled down to my throat, to the top of my breast as he quickly helped me take off my clothes—the dress I'd thrown on without thinking, my tacky, unmatched silk panties and bra—removing them and savoring each part of me that their removal revealed. I helped him take off his trousers and then his shirt, still damp from the rain, and when we kissed again, it was I who took the initiative, my lips grazing his face, touching his neck, feeling the rough edge of his beard against my lips and cheek, and then feeling his response as strong and demanding as my own. His lips, tongue, and fingers searched me where they could, exploring what they could of my body as eagerly as I had his.

His body was as beautiful as I remembered it—the broad, strong shoulders, slender waist, and solid, powerful thighs of a runner. There was a raised, jagged scar that ran the length of his left shoulder down toward his heart, and I touched it, curious.

"A jealous woman's knife," he mumbled shyly, with a mixture of embarrassment and amused pride. He lifted my hand from it, as if I'd struck some unpleasant memory, and sucked the tips of my fingers. I ran my lips over the smooth, flawless skin of his back, shoulders, and then he drew me to him, kissing my throat and the back of my neck, his tongue pushing into my mouth and playing with the tip of mine. Our bodies came together in a sudden rush of shared, frantic excitement. He caressed and then kissed my back, breast, and between my thighs, lingering teasingly, and I felt myself grow weak with desire for him. I was swept up, drunk with every part of him, the way he felt, his smell, his taste.

But then I stopped and pulled away, catching my breath. As many times as I'd warned my son about "being prepared" and cautioned him about "getting caught up in the moment," here I was doing just that.

"They're in the drawer, the second one down, next to you," Basil muttered, as if reading my mind. I rolled over and reached toward the small bedstand at my side, as he ran his fingers as lightly as a feather up and down my spine.

I was in a daze from his touch. It took me a moment to realize that I'd opened the wrong drawer, and there were no condoms there. But there was a gun, a stubby black one—an ugly, brutal affront to my passion. I drew away from it, repulsed by its presence. Basil sat up slightly and leaned over me, getting the condoms from the proper drawer, kissing my shoulder and slamming the drawer closed in one fluid motion.

"It shouldn't surprise you. You know who I am," he murmured as he pulled me on top of him, awakening my passion again with a shower of swift, strong kisses.

But I didn't know who he was. Not really. Even as his lips spread pleasure wherever they touched me, even as I was lost in the lingering scent of him, and in the tart, salty taste of his skin upon my tongue, I knew there were parts of him that I would never know. I knew that he would always be a mystery to me, even as he thrust himself into me more deeply than any man before him, and as we surrendered ourselves to each other with delirious abandon.

13

We had awakened at dawn, made love in a room washed pink with early morning light, and drifted back to sleep. I awoke now to the sound of two people arguing in an angry mix of patois and English, the woman screaming so loud and talking so fast I couldn't make out a word she was saying. Her young, shrill voice made me think of Lilah, and I felt a sudden sadness, as if something between us had been left undone. Still in a daze, I threw my hand to Basil's side of the bed, which was empty. Fully awake, I got up and padded across the tiled floor and out to the terrace.

The green-and-purple mountains loomed as far as I could see. The sky looked bluer than I'd ever remembered seeing it, and the sun beamed down hard on the terrace, making everything hot to the touch. I stepped back inside, took a quick shower in the bathroom down the hall, and pulled on my underwear and dress, mildly disgusted that I had to wear yesterday's clothes. Basil walked in behind me as I dressed and kissed me twice on the nape of my neck, sending a quick, hot thrill down the center of my spine.

"So you heard us this morning, her screaming at me like that," he said as he sat down on the bed. "We were fighting about her lover. Her involvement with him leaves me vulnerable."

"Leaves *you* vulnerable?" It struck me as odd that his sister's boyfriend could make him feel threatened.

"Believe me, you don't want to know all the ins and outs of it," he said, in a way that told me to leave it alone. "I don't know who she is anymore, what she has become," he added more introspectively. "There is a hardness that has settled in her. Maybe he put it there, maybe it was always there and I never saw it.

"We're going to have to leave for Kingston shortly, Bettina and me, like I mentioned last night," he continued. "It's a matter regarding my mother's estate, small though it was. My mother left a little money in a savings account, and it will take both our signatures to secure it. I want to make sure it goes to her grandsons, and not into the wrong greedy hands."

"You're going now?" I didn't mean to whine out the words like a disappointed teenager, but that was how they came out.

"Bettina insists upon leaving tomorrow. Today is the only day left. I'll be back in an hour. Two at most. Don't worry."

"I'm not worried," I quickly added, not wanting to sound dependent, like a needy woman.

He kissed me lightly on the throat and then the lips, lingering as if teasing me with what might yet come. "There's a pool down from the house, and a garden. It's beautiful. Restful. Go back to sleep. It's still early."

"As long as you're not too long. I don't want to be hanging around too long. I want to catch that plane back. Take care of *my* business."

"You won't be, but I was hoping to tempt you to stay here with me for a while. Think about it."

"I don't know—"

"Yes you do."

"But I'd planned—"

"What?" he asked, his eyes sparkling with amusement. "What could be better than this?"

I had to smile at the truth of that.

"We don't know when we will be together again."

That was for sure. It seemed like it had taken me half my adult life to finally hop into bed with the man, and the leap had definitely been worth the wait.

"There is more to this island than Kingston," he continued. "You've seen nothing—all the problems, none of the pleasures. Don't go back yet."

"Well—"

"I can rent a car in Kingston, drive back here. We can go back to your hotel room, take care of the bill, pick up what you need, then drive north up the coast to Port Antonio. I have a friend who manages a place on the beach. We can go from there to Ocho Rios, if you want, and then to Negril. Montego Bay. Where the rich and famous spend their money."

It was sounding good.

"I want to show you my country, Tamara, the way that it should be shown, the way I love it. Take a plane home from Montego Bay. Talk to the woman at the embassy, tell her you met up with a friend, a long-lost cousin of your mother's or something, and he is taking good care of you, and that the passport people can give you what you need in Montego Bay. Believe me, you'll have less trouble from there than Kingston. The farther away you are from all that has happened, the better off you will be."

A smile found its way to my lips. It's always amazing how quickly good sex will make a bad week gleam with possibility.

"Tamara—"

"I don't have any money," I interrupted.

"You don't *need* any money."

"I don't like being dependent on you." But considering what I'd been for the last twenty-four hours, that probably sounded silly.

"I'll make you a loan, Tamara, if that's what it takes. Listen, accept this gift with grace. Taking something from someone who wants to give it is as much a virtue as giving to one who needs. Take this one from me, I want to give it."

What was there to keep me back? I could call Annie and Jamal and tell them that things had worked out and I was going to stay down for the rest of my vacation after all. I could even pick up Annie's money in Kingston at a Western Union when I picked up my suitcase, and then buy the ticket in Montego Bay like he said. Basil was right about one thing: it would be wise to put distance between myself and Kingston.

"Yeah, maybe so," I answered myself. "Okay."

It was good to feel like a tourist again as we strolled downstairs. Better than feeling like prey.

A young woman with hair elaborately braided into what Wyvetta Green would call goddess braids, was sitting on the terrace with her back to me. She was tiny, no bigger than a girl, and when she glanced to the side, her profile was like Basil's. At long last, I was going to meet his sister Bettina.

The slight, almost imperceptible shift of her head, like that of a skittish animal who picks up a predator's scent, told me that she'd heard us coming. She placed her coffee cup down on the table and sat very straight, not acknowledging me until I was in her view. I thought of what Basil's mother had said about her, and the cruel detachment with which those words must have been spoken. This mother had not been a tender woman, and she had passed it down. Every movement her daughter made spoke anger; there seemed to be no spare kindness in her small, thin frame.

Basil, obviously unwilling to go another round, had left for another part of the house. I walked around the table and sat down. Her look of annoyance made me wonder if I had blocked her view.

"Good morning," I said cheerfully, sounding like a program director on a second-rate cruise ship. She looked me up and down, then nodded toward the cup that sat near me.

"Blue Mountain," she finally said, in a low voice that sounded as if it shouldn't come from her face. I was puzzled for moment, and then assumed she was nodding toward the mountains in the distance.

"They're beautiful. I've never seen anything—"

"Not the mountains, the coffee." She didn't add "you fool" but it was clearly intended. "You can't get it easily in the States. Only the rich drink it here. Drink what you can while you can get it." She didn't say it nastily, but rather in a no-nonsense, matter-of-fact way, as if she was telling me something that she thought I should know.

It *was* Blue Mountain coffee. The real thing. I sipped it for a while in appreciative silence, savoring the aroma as only a true coffee lover can, enjoying a sense of well-being as the familiar jolt of caffeine charged through me.

She was clearly a woman who, as my grandma would say, kept her own counsel; it was impossible to tell what was on her mind as she studied me over her cup.

"You are an American who is visiting my brother, right?" she finally said. There was a surprising jerkiness to her words as she asked the question, a nervousness that hinted at both fear and insecurity.

"Yes," I answered curtly, startled by the way she'd said it.

"You must not be of much importance. He's never mentioned you to me. I've never heard of you," she said with casual cruelty. I was taken aback.

"I wish I could say the same about you." It was nasty and I knew it, but it had hit home. Her mouth dropped slightly and her eyes shifted from mine. But I was surprised by the look of pain that flitted across her face, and in the next moment ashamed for using something like that, which may have been told in confidence, against her. Maybe she wasn't as hard as she wanted people to think.

"He reminds me of my brother," I said after a moment, deciding to give us both a chance to seek some common ground.

"My brother does?"

I nodded, and her face softened suddenly, but then she pulled her muscles tight again, concealing anything that the softness might reveal.

She did look amazingly like Basil, with the same high cheekbones, soft, sensual lips and skin nearly the same color as the rich coffee in our cups. But she had a widow's peak that gave her heart-shaped face a sweetness his didn't have, and there was that innocence that Basil had mentioned. I thought about the corrupting influence of my charming, ne'er-do-well ex-husband, DeWayne Curtis, and I felt strangely ashamed and guilty, as if by simple association I had played a part in her fate. I thought about the smiling young girl whose fresh face peeked out from a locket that Basil had once worn around his neck. Perhaps he had told me the truth after all; that young girl was as dead as he'd said.

"My brother didn't like my boyfriends either," I said, jumping to that common ground again.

"So what's he say about Basil, this brother of yours?"

"He's dead."

"So what happened to him?"

I paused for a moment like I always do before I say it, then deciding to go on with it anyway.

"He killed himself." The look that I get whenever I say those words came to her face and left. She glanced away.

"That must have been rough."

"It's still rough."

"So Basil reminds you of your brother, you say? But I don't think he would do something like that."

"No, I don't think he would. He's too tough."

"So yours wasn't tough?"

"What killed him was tougher."

"What was it?"

"I only wish I knew."

She had softened although you couldn't hear it in her voice. It was in those eyes, deep and sad and so much like Basil's. I tried to place her age. Mid to late twenties maybe. A couple of years older than Lilah. A couple of years harder.

"Want more coffee?" She pushed the pot over toward me, a peace offering. "They say it's the best coffee in the world."

"I should drink what I can while I can get it." She smiled when I said it, as if we'd crossed some invisible barrier.

"You heard us fighting then."

"I used to fight with my brother like that. Loved him but fought with him. Half the time I didn't feel like he understood me. I know how much he loved me, though. Like big brothers do. Like yours loves you."

She looked at me as if she didn't know what I was talking about.

"That girl he loved is dead, like her mother," she said finally. "I came home to bury what was left of her. I'm here because my mother is dead, for no other reason. I despise this place. It disgusts me. The squalor. The filth." She said it evenly, the contempt cutting through each of her words.

"This is a beautiful country, Bettina. It's part of you and your family. Hold your head high. You should be proud of it!" I kept my tone friendly, not scolding.

"Who the bloody hell do you think you are, telling me how to feel or what I should think of this country? You spend a night fucking my brother and think you know about me and my family and what I should feel?" She spat the words out with a venom that felt like a slap; the rage seemed to erupt from nowhere. I stared at her, stunned, wondering what in the hell I'd said to bring on a response like that.

"I'm sorry, Bettina," I managed to mutter.

"Let me tell you something, American bitch who fucks my brother. Don't be sorry for me. Never be sorry for me," she said with nothing in her eyes.

"Honey, you don't have to worry about that," I snapped back when I found my voice. I had wanted to like her because of my relationship to her brother, but the last thing I needed this morning was a bitch before breakfast. I picked up my cup and moved to another part of the terrace.

"Bettina, come now!" Basil ordered from inside the house. His voice was stiff and unnatural, and I wondered if he'd heard our exchange. Without saying anything else she rose.

"So you'll be here?" she asked over her shoulder as she left. Was she interested, curious, or did she think I was going to rob the place while they were away? She didn't wait around for an answer, and I didn't bother to give one.

I took a deep breath, and let it out slowly.

"Goddamn," I said aloud, but then in the same breath I muttered a quiet, "Let it go." Whatever it was that had given the woman such an attitude, it wasn't my problem. I've lived long enough to know not to grab somebody else's baggage, my own is heavy enough, and this was one suitcase that definitely didn't belong to me. But Bettina had soured my good spirits, and I suddenly felt mean and slightly depressed. The sun was getting hotter, so I left the terrace and went inside the house.

Don't take it to heart, I told myself. I thought about Port Antonio, and tried to put the nasty exchange with Bettina out of my mind. But there was something disturbing about it and her that I couldn't quite put my finger on. Basil had been right about her. What had she become?

"Let it go, Tamara," I actually said out loud, cautioning myself not to obsess about it. And besides that, I reminded myself, now that I was alone I could openly satisfy my curiosity about this place. I'd actually seen very little of it—some of the terrace, a bit of the living room, most of Basil's bedroom. That was one thing I could do to get even, snoop around the house to see what I could find out about her. Being nosy, I'm ashamed to admit, has always been my downfall.

I wandered through the living room first, and then into the neat, narrow kitchen, with its double window over the sink that looked out to the backyard. It was obviously the kind of place that one needed "help" to take care of, as the rich folks would put it. Someone probably came in to do the heavy cleaning, and from the look of the dishes piled in the sink, today was apparently her day off. Bettina didn't strike me as the kind of sister who would pick up a broom, and Basil was definitely not a dust-mopping kind of brother.

The kitchen's back door opened to a ragged path that led to stone stairs going up a small incline to a garden and pool that looked overgrown and uncared for. A white cement bench that looked like it came from somebody's London garden stood on the far edge of the pool, from where you could look back and clearly see the kitchen door and windows.

But the pool looked like it hadn't been used in months. Moss grew everywhere, and the water was covered with green scum. A swarm of mosquitoes who had claimed it as their own buzzed around my head. It was hot as hell, but a dip was definitely out of the question. The area behind the bench was overgrown with trees, thick vegetation, and odd, fetid flowers that sprouted wildly and seemed to be rotting from the heat. The quick, high squawk of a bird gave the place an eerie feel. A huge, slimy lizard darted out of nowhere and scampered over my big toe. I quickly made my way back to the safety of the house, slamming the door behind me.

I felt silly when I got inside and was glad I was alone. If Jamal had seen me, I'd be hearing about it for the next fifteen years. But I wasn't about to go outside again. I started looking for a TV to pass the time, but could find neither that, a radio, nor the boom box that Basil had played last night. I also looked for a phone. There was one in the living room, but the line was dead. Anxiety swept me, and I pushed it down, not allowing it to take root.

The house was larger than I'd thought at first, and its emptiness added to its size. The dark wood, which had given the place such a romantic glow in the lamplight last night, gave it a melancholy feel in the day. The place seemed almost grotesque, a gloomy parody of a rich man's home. I wondered again about the owner and the things Basil had told me about him.

I wandered back into the kitchen and opened the refrigerator, looking for something to eat. The coffee had been good, but not that good. Hunger was starting to get the better of me.

There was a blue china bowl filled with oranges and lemons on the top shelf that looked like it had been snatched from the pages of *Gourmet*. I've never been one to resist the call of food, especially when it's fat, and guilt free, so I grabbed an orange and peeled it, jamming the sweet tangy fruit into my mouth. When I'd finished, juice and pulp dripping down my lips and my chin, I looked for a napkin or paper towel but couldn't find one, so I turned on the tap of the kitchen sink, bending over and splashing water on my face and hands.

I looked in the refrigerator for something to drink and found an opened bakery box filled with meat patties, one of which was calling my name. It was close to noon, so I ate one, calling it lunch, with a slight but brief feeling of guilt knowing that I was eating somebody else's food; but the guilt didn't stop me from gobbling down another. I grabbed a Red Stripe beer from among the half-dozen that were on the shelf, looked for a can opener and found one in the bottom of the sink under the dishes and a rusty butcher knife. I opened it and sat down to sip it. My animal hunger sated, I began to think again about last night.

No regrets. Whatever happened after today, after he returned, after Port Antonio, Negril, or wherever else we ended up, I would have no regrets. Nothing could take away last night.

I will have no regrets. I repeated the words to myself, wondering why it even occurred to me that there should be any. I never seem to be able to relax into happiness, to take joy as my right, and I scolded myself for it. Why couldn't I accept happiness as my due? I laughed at myself, amused but feeling better. Almost content.

"Enjoy it, Tam!" I actually said aloud. "Enjoy it! No regrets!" *It must be the Red Stripe,* I thought to myself. Considering how tense and apprehensive I'd felt a few moments ago, maybe a bottle of beer on a nearly empty stomach was just what I needed.

I'm not sure what sudden instinct made me glance up, what second sense had intruded into my good spirits. A man stared at me through the kitchen window. I grabbed my mouth with my hand, stifling my scream, my eyes darting to the kitchen door to check the bolt that was, of course, unlocked. He seemed to read my mind as he jammed his huge hand inside the door to keep me from locking it. He stepped inside. I stepped back.

His beaked cap was pulled down low over his homely face, partially concealing it, but I could see his sleepy eyes, pretty but as cold and empty as an animal's; they seemed to look straight through me. He was a big man, dressed in a tan cotton vest worn without a shirt, which revealed the muscles in his arms and chest as big as those of some freak in a traveling circus. A thin gold chain sparkled on his chest.

It isn't Lacey. It took that simple thought a moment to register, but there was something about his stance, how quickly that big hand had grabbed the door, that terrified me. He saw, smelled my fear.

"Who the hell are you and what are you doing in my brother's house?" His voice was deep, menacing, and the rhythm of it told me he was Jamaican, but he spoke with a British accent, a pretentious one that was phony, annoying. *Scratch.* I nearly said the name but then hesitated, wondering if they called him that to his face. Scratch. An old name for a goblin. The devil. What kind of an evil kid would cause his playmates to give him a nickname like that? I knew now what had been in Bettina's voice when she asked if I'd be here. She must have been expecting him.

"I asked you a question."

This *was* his brother's house. He had more right here than me. I smiled, and stepped back. I wasn't big enough to keep him out if he wanted to come in. Smarter to play the nonthreatening, unassuming little woman.

"I'm sorry. You startled me. I'm a friend of—of Bettina's," I stuttered out. Better not mention Basil. I could only assume that their feelings toward each other were mutual. "I'm visiting from the States," I babbled on, risking the possibility that he would assume that I made my living like Bettina did. But the way his eyes roamed my body, checking me out like a piece of jerk chicken, made it clear that he had assumed it. I tried to think of something to say to clean it up and came up blank.

"A friend of Bettina's?"

"From the States," I lied on, digging myself in deeper.

"When?"

"When what?"

"When did you get in?"

"This morning."

"There are no planes from the States this early."

"I said I knew her from the States, not that I just came in from there. I got here, to this place, early this morning." I didn't like the way he was cross-examining me but I kept my voice even and friendly.

"Where you know her from?"

"Newark." I offered up the name of my hometown, the first thing that came to my mind.

"You look familiar."

"I have one of those faces people say that about," I said, moving toward the open door as he came forward, the two of us switching places.

"No. I know you." He nodded his head like he was trying to shake up a thought, studying me, trying to place me, and that pricked the voice inside me that warns me, because he looked familiar too—those hollow eyes did.

"She left something for me?"

My mind went blank, and I wondered for one horrible moment if he was talking about that box of meat patties I'd helped myself to. But then I realized it was something else. He was testing me.

"She said to expect you," I said, hoping that would take care of it.

"Where did she say it was?"

"She don't tell nobody shit, you know that if you know Bettina," I said, taking a chance, and he smiled, telling me I'd played it right. "Bettina don't tell nobody shit." I forced a laugh, but it came out high and false from the top of my throat. "She just said you were coming by. Her mother croaked. She had to take care of some business."

"By herself?"

"No, with somebody else. Some big guy. Jamaican. Said he was her brother."

"That black bastard."

"Like I said, I just got here."

He opened the refrigerator and pulled out a bottle of Red Stripe. I halfway expected him to open it with his teeth, but he took a long pocketknife from his pocket and flicked it open. The blade was ugly—long and serrated on the edges; it was like the kind a hunter uses to cut and dress his game. He nicked off the cap with the blade and licked the foam from the top of the bottle as he turned to face me.

"So you with Bettina, eh?"

"That's what I said."

He chuckled as if he knew I was lying. He tossed the beer down in several loud gulps and slammed the bottle into the sink, shattering it to pieces. The sudden, unexpected violence of it unnerved me, and he glanced at me scornfully, like some mean kid who pulls the wings off flies to make his sister cry.

Perhaps Bettina's mother had been right about her after all. A woman who could be with a man like this must have part of him within her, too. But how much of Sammy Lee had been in Lilah? How much of my ex-husband had been in me? Maybe I was judging him too quickly, taking Basil too much at his word.

Scratch. Yet even saying the name to myself made me nervous, scared like I'd been when I was a kid and my grandmother would say that name when she talked about the devil. *Old Scratch scratching at your soul.*

"I left something outside." My voice was tight as I struggled to keep the tremble out of it, and I stared at the wall over his head as I said it, not wanting to look at his face. I wondered if he noticed.

He shrugged indifferently. "Don't get bit by no snakes out there," he said, with malicious amusement that made me wonder if he had been watching when I'd been chased back into the house by the lizard.

I didn't know, but I walked briskly out the kitchen door, over the

154

path, down to the pool, and dropped down on the stone bench facing the house. He watched me from the window, and I kept my eyes on him too. Don't *never* turn your back on a stray dog, my grandma told me once, and I took her advice, studying him so closely I missed the furtive movement in the bushes behind the bench.

14

Suddenly someone stood behind me. He jerked my head straight back by my hair. I could smell the acrid, bitter stink of sweat and dust that came from him. He pulled me so close I thought I would be sick. I was conscious of nothing but that my breath was caught in the back of my throat with a scream.

This is how it feels to die.

The thought broke through half formed, along with the sound of that high squeak of a voice I thought I'd left in Kingston.

"I'm gonna break it, bitch," Lacey said. "You want me to break your goddamn neck? Tell me what you did with the goddamn money? Making me climb up that damn hill like that. Climbing up from that damn road through all this shit. Where is my goddamn money?"

He let me go then, and my head swung forward. I saw the sun in blinding brightness and felt a humiliating sense of gratitude to him for taking away that choking death he had the power to inflict.

I was sure for a moment that I heard the sound of Basil's motor-bike. It seemed far away as it came up the road. But then the hum faded. Did he park it? I wondered. Was he going into that house? Or was my mind playing games with me? Was this its way of protecting me from what was happening to me? If it was Basil, he'd be out here, I knew that for sure.

But nobody came. Not even Scratch. I looked at the window, but he was nowhere to be seen, and a sense of alarm raced through me. I cursed the luck that made my survival dependent upon *Scratch's* goodwill, and I came back to what I could feel—Lacey's hand knotted in my hair, tugging it hard with each word he spoke, and my eyes watering from fear and pain.

"I don't want to hurt you none. I don't want to but I will. I just want you to tell me where my money is, and I'll be on my way. I don't believe in hurting no pretty woman."

He yanked twice, hard. "I need it. Can't you understand that? It don't belong to you. Hell, it don't even belong to me, but I guess I have as much right to it as anybody else."

"How did you find me?" He held my head tight against his chest. I could feel the sweat pouring off my face, dripping down my neck and making it itch.

"I got my ways." He laughed, but then, as if taking pity on me for some reason, he explained quickly. "It was in the bag. That black traveling bag your girlfriend saw me with over Delaware's."

Maybe if I talked to him, stalled him, I could figure out what to do. I tested his hold on me, pulling away slightly, tucking in my chin, but he snatched me back. I let my head go where he wanted it to, not fighting back, surrendering.

"In the black traveling bag?" I asked.

"You know which one I'm talking about."

"The one that Lilah had? The one she had over Delaware's?" I was guessing, repeating what he'd said, taking a chance that he wouldn't notice.

"The one you got now. Heinz 57 wrote the address to this place on a scrap of paper. Son of a bitch forgot to take it out, I guess. I found it over Delaware's that night when we was going through that bag and stuffed it in my pocket. Figured you never know when something like that, an address with no name, hidden in a pocket in something like that will come in handy. I didn't even know you were going to be here. That scrap of paper was all I had. I figured if I followed it, sooner or later it might lead me to the money. Looks like it did. I came up by the back if that's what you want to know. Won't do you no good to know it now, though." He was full of himself now, bragging, showing off.

I reached for his hands, grabbing for his wrists with clawed hands, my nails tearing into the flesh on his fingers and wrists. He squealed in surprise but then jerked my head again and I let go, screaming as the streak of pain traveled down from my skull into my eyes and settled in my neck. I saw only darkness for a moment, as if my head had been slammed into a hole. He snatched me back again, rocking me against him. The muscles in my neck were so tight I couldn't breathe.

"Didn't you hear me?" he demanded. "Didn't you hear me ask you about that money? Don't make me hurt you."

"All right then! I'll tell you," I shrieked. The voice wasn't mine; it came from somewhere dark and scared inside me where I'd never been before. "I'll tell you what you need to know, just let me go. Please, let me go."

He paused a moment, and then let my hair go. He came around the bench, stood in front of me wearing a sloppy grin of triumph. I stood to face him. I wanted to spit in his face. I bit my bottom lip hard to keep from doing it, afraid to trust myself. Sweat dripped down his angular, unshaven face, putting a shine on his pockmarked skin and blending with the dust that covered him and the disheveled T-shirt and jeans he wore. His hazel eyes were squinted and hateful. I closed my eyes so I wouldn't look into them. I took a breath, held it for a minute and let it go, pulling myself back together, praying to every ancestor I'd ever heard of to get me through this. Then I opened my eyes and faced him, taking his measure, deciding in that moment what I would do and how I would do it.

"What you doing down here mixed up in something like this anyway?" he said, his voice gone soft, almost sympathetic. He thought I had given up, submitted to his will. I knew I could use that against him. "You don't look like the kind of woman who would be involved with something like that. You look like you're smart. Pretty." He stroked the side of my face. "You should know you can't fight—" He stopped short as I rocked back, my face empty of expression, my eyes rolling back in my head and twitching as if I was going to faint. He grabbed me to keep me from falling, which told me more about him than he knew.

"Don't be passing out on me, baby. Don't be having no fainting spell and shit, until you told me what I have to know." He spoke softly, with a plea in his voice, but there was also a threat.

He shook me hard, shaking me until my head knocked against my chin. I pulled away and shifted forward a bit, unsteadily, like I was drunk. I dropped down and doubled up, pulling the muscles in my stomach and neck as tight as I could get them. I made a mewling sigh as if I were in pain, placing my hands on my knees, bracing myself to give myself as much support as I could. He watched me in amazement, not sure what to make of me. I started to gag, slobber dripping from my mouth, heaving and pitching forward and back as if I had lost control and was getting ready to vomit or have some kind of a fit.

"Oh, Jesus," he said in disgust. "What the fuck—" He backed out of my way, closer to the pool, letting his hands drop away from me to his sides. It was then that I made my move. I reared back as far as I could and in the same motion butted him hard with my head, using it like a battering ram, slamming him once and then again in his groin, knocking the breath out of him and ramming him with every bit of strength that was in me, every bit of will I had left. My head hurt like hell from the impact.

With a yelp of pain and surprise, he fell backward, his thin frame nearly toppling into the water, but then he caught himself like a clumsy acrobat. Trying to keep his balance, he pitched forward to keep from going into the pool, and then fell flat on his stomach near its edge, his arms splayed out on either side. He glanced up, his eyes big with surprise, a curse on his lips as he moved fast, trying to stand up quickly. But I moved faster, landing with all my weight on his back, shoving one knee deep into his spine and the other between his shoulder blades, riding across his back like he was a sled heading down a hill. He bolted forward, and for one scary moment I thought we'd both topple into the pool, but dumb luck was with me again. He gave a howl, as he tried to get up while grabbing me, but I kept my knee pressed hard against his shoulder blades, making it impossible for him to move freely.

His head had dropped to where I wanted it, just high enough above and close enough to the mucky water. I grabbed him by the hair, and shoved his face in. I was breathing evenly again, even though my neck still hurt. My instincts had kicked back in.

"You fucking bitch! What the hell did you do that for?" he squealed when I brought his head up again. He shook it from side to side like a dog coming out of a lake as he tried to shake my hands off. Saliva spluttered from his mouth as he spat twice, trying not to swallow the scummy water he'd taken in. He tried to snatch my hands and then wiggle his back to shake me off, but I was on him like a tick, as fixed to him as white on rice. I dunked his head again, counting to ten this time before I let him back up.

"Ooh, Jesus," he screamed out.

"That's for pulling my hair like you did just now, you lousy son of a bitch," I said, and dunked him again. "And that's for scaring the shit out of me on the phone the other night. I am not mixed up in this mess or that money you keep talking about. I met those people at the hotel. They took me out for a drink. Next thing I knew they started dying. I don't have your goddamn money. I never had your goddamn money. I don't want your goddamn money. I don't even know what goddamn money you're talking about." I was breathing hard again, my words pouring out in a tirade.

"Ooh, God." He spat out water and bucked, squirming on the dirt like a worm, trying to toss me over his head. I pulled his head up, arching his neck the way he had mine, and dunked him again. He gasped and sputtered.

"And that's for Lilah Love," I said, my rage finally spent.

"I told you before, I don't know nothing about no damn Lilah Love," he said between gasps.

I settled onto him, my bony knees lodged deep into points on his lean back, still holding his hair. He made another grab for my legs, but I moved quickly, and he finally gave up. His nose had begun to bleed, and I watched the blood drip off his face and run in a red line into the green water.

"Put your hands up where I can see them," I said. "Up above your head, into the pool."

He didn't move, and I yanked his hair again, hard enough for him to know I wasn't playing.

"Let me up, girl. Let me up!"

"What happened to 'bitch'? Not on your life."

He lay there for a moment catching his breath. Finally, he moved his skinny arms slowly over his head, his fingers touching the surface of the pool. He seemed weak now, harmless. But I'd run into many a fool who seemed helpless until you let down your guard. I tightened my grip on his hair.

"I want it all now."

"What the fuck are you talking about? Girl, if I—"

"Call me Ms. Hayle, asshole. I want it all."

"What all?"

"Starting with the money and Heinz 57."

"Go fuck yourself."

I dunked him again.

"It was the money he'd put in that bag. Heinz put the money in his bag."

"Who the hell is Heinz 57?"

"Was Heinz 57. He's dead now."

"That was his name?"

"I don't know what his name was, and if I'd asked he probably wouldn't have told it. He didn't mind me calling him Heinz, so that's what I called him. Heinz 57. He didn't call me by my right name either."

"I asked you who he was."

"He was that German guy standing by the bar, when you came in there with Delaware. That's who he was."

I eased up, shifting back slightly. All the fight had gone out of him.

I tried to recall the scene in the Stamp and Go. We'd entered the bar, Delaware had called out to Lacey, and we'd gone to where they stood. Lacey. The German. The dude who Sammy Lee had bullied and who the drink had been spilled on. There had been a squat black duffel bag sitting on the floor between Lacey and the German. That must have been the black traveling bag Lacey was talking about. It had struck me as strange then, how incongruous it was, a duffel bag in a place like that, as if the owner was going somewhere fast.

"So you knew him? This Heinz?"

"We'd done some business before, laid some plans. I saw him down in Negril last week sometime. He asked me for some help. Said he was going to the States, and would be coming back to Jamaica this week. He was bringing back something to give to somebody in Kingston. Asked if I'd come along. Make sure things went all right. He'd give me a couple of grand for my trouble, he said. I went along."

I thought about my deal with Lilah. Greed will get you every time.

"Why don't you get off my back?" he yelped, starting to bounce again. "You ain't no little baby, you know, and I ain't exactly a mound of flesh. You liable to break my back. Get off my damn back!"

"So you can throw me in the pool? Who was he meeting?"

He started to squirm again. "Hell if I know. Somebody."

"Sammy Lee said he knew you. Did you know him?"

He didn't say anything for a minute. I jerked his head.

"I knowed Sammy Lee Love back in the day. Back in Jersey City. We used to call him Lee, just plain Lee. I used to run with one of his boys who turned on him, done him real wrong. That's where he knew me from. Sure I remembered him, but I didn't own up to it. I didn't even know Delaware knew the man till I saw him in there that night." He lunged forward, but I held on tightly.

"Get off my goddamn back! I'm not going to hurt you. If I was going to hurt you, I woulda done it when I first grabbed your hair. I ain't into hurting pretty women."

"Just snatching their heads off. Go on, I want to get this straight."

"Why you want to get it straight? If you don't know nothing about that money, why's it so damn important to you? I thought you said you didn't hardly know them anyway."

"Two men and a young woman are dead over it," I said. Basil was right about me. It always came down to my sense of justice. I needed to know what it was really about. Maybe it was the cop in me. Maybe it was just that they all owed me something even if it just came down to an explanation for what had happened. I had to make some sense of it.

"Dead is dead."

"So I want to know why it happened."

"So get off my back."

"Get this straight. We're not talking about me getting off your back. We're talking about you not drinking any more of that water."

"Why should I tell you shit?"

"Suit yourself. But I have some friends who will be coming back soon here. In fact, the owner of the place is in there now, he is the kind of guy you do not want to mess with, and we'll turn you over to these Jamaican cops—and from what I hear about these brothers, they make those chumps in the LAPD look like Eagle Scouts. I know you were mixed up in all this dying that's been going on. If you tell me, I'll get up. I won't tell my friends you're here. You can crawl back into the hole you crawled out of with your balls still intact."

He thought for a moment. "So where are these friends?"

"One's in the house."

"So how come he ain't out here looking out for you?"

"He knows I can take care of myself."

That was bullshit, and I hoped he couldn't tell it. I didn't have any friend in the house, and I didn't know what the hell my next move was going to be. If that motorcycle I thought I'd heard had been Basil, he would have been out here by now. So I knew I would still have to wait some for him to get back. I also knew that sooner or later I'd have to get off the man's back. Maybe it would come down to Scratch. He was one big, evil-looking dude, and Lacey was on his brother's property with less right to be here even than me. Sooner or later he would come out here to check things out. Lacey would be more fun for him to bully than me, if for no other reason than to see the fear in his hazel eyes. Then maybe I could get up, and let the two of them duke it out. Maybe.

"He'll be out here soon enough," I said, glancing up to the house. Scratch was nowhere to be seen, but it seemed to give Lacey pause.

"I don't know shit. But what you want to know?" he asked after a minute.

"What was the money for?"

"Hell if I know. Drugs. That's big around here now. Puerto Rico. Mexico. All the big boys done put Colombia down, they're fooling around the islands these days."

"Who was he bringing it to?"

"I told you. It was going from the States to some dude in that place where all this shit jumped off. Payment for something. I don't know for what. He said to meet this dude in the club, and that's what I did. Heinz was carrying it for somebody, taking it to somebody in that club."

"So you knew this German before?"

"You ain't hearing things too tough, are you, baby? I told you, yeah. I hang around. Do some shit. A little dab here, a little dab there. I'm legit sometimes though. Sometimes not so legit. So I knew this guy. Heinz. Met him in Antigua a couple of years ago. So he told me to go with him to this place to meet this dude. We'd both been there before, but not enough for anybody except the bartender to know us, and we knew he wouldn't say nothing. Heinz had told me to pretend we didn't know each other, so we didn't say nothing to each other. It would work better that way, he said. I was just going to check out the dude and make sure he wasn't packin', which I did, and he wasn't. Heinz said something wasn't smelling right to him. He wanted to have me there for protection. Because maybe this guy he was meeting wouldn't want him hanging around. I don't know why. That's what he said. You can't trust any of these bastards.

"And then my boy Delaware Brown comes in, all the way from Jersey City, and that little fox started snapping those pictures. Last damn thing I wanted to happen, standing there with Heinz and shit. The lights got shot out. I grabbed that bag of money. I ran."

He was vague about the details, but I sensed he was telling me the truth. He was one of those men who live on the edge of virtue, selling their souls to the hand flashing the most cash or the one squeezing his balls, or in my case yanking his hair. When it came down, I sensed he didn't have enough heart to lie.

"So you killed the German and took his bag filled with money?"

I said it even though I was sure that he didn't have the stomach to kill anybody. Not the German. Or for that matter, Lilah, Delaware Brown, or me.

"I told you once, I didn't kill nobody. Those little hoodlums shot out those lights. Heinz fell all up against me. There was enough light coming up through that door to see the man was dead, blood coming out him. When he fell, his knees got knocked out from under him and he slid down. He knocked that bag right under my feet, the thing was just begging for me to pick it up, so I did. Took it by Delaware's room later on that night. Left it there with him."

"Hold it. You're saying that you left that bag at Delaware Brown's?"

"Yeah."

"How much money was in it?"

He paused. "More than I like to think about. More than I'll ever see again," he added wistfully. "It wasn't just cash though. It was bonds, bearer's bonds I think they call them. Big denominations. Some cash, small bills."

"Why did you leave it with Delaware?"

"There was too much damn money to be hauling around by myself. Hell, that German had enough sense to have me riding backup, be damned if I wouldn't need some too. Now that I knew how much was in it. Didn't make no sense, carrying it nowhere. Kingston's got as bad as New York City when it comes to youngbloods ripping you off. I didn't know if anybody'd seen me with it or not. I knowed Delaware a long time. Knew I could trust him. We always been like brothers.

"I left it there, with him in that room. Saw him put it in a closet. I came back the next morning, early, to pick it up and split some of it with him for keeping it for me. But somebody had knocked that boy dead, straight through his head. I figured it was one of you all. That

girl Lilah, the one who took the pictures, was there when we were talking about it. I figured the money was with her. Then when I went by
where she stayed and they told me the cops were sniffing around her
room, I figured it might be with you, 'cause you were with them.
That's why I called you looking for it. I seen you all together, so I
thought you were in it together."

"Lilah was there when you were there? When you showed
Delaware the money?"

But I knew that she had been.

*Somebody came by. They talked for a while, and then the guy left,
and Delaware got agitated and mad all over again, and I got out of there
fast.*

I had sensed she was lying when she'd said it, and I knew it now.
She'd conveniently forgotten to mention the money this visitor had
brought and left in Delaware's room, the money she must have gone
back to get because she knew it was still there, that whoever killed
Delaware hadn't gotten it. But it hadn't belonged to her any more than
it had belonged to Delaware or Lacey or probably even the man it was
intended for. "All that loot" had probably killed her.

"I never had the money," I said. "And if Lilah had it, she doesn't
have it now."

"Something ain't adding up here," Lacey said. "Ain't that much
money gone somewhere without somebody knowing where it's at."

But it was beginning to make sense to me now, and I put it together,
remembering faces, words, and actions.

"Somebody does," I answered him. "It's come full circle. It's back
with the man who was supposed to get it from the German in the first
place. The only one down here who knew kids poor enough to shoot
off guns for cash so he could take out somebody because he had no
more use for him. He knew you took that black bag of cash and bonds,
and he knew where to find Delaware Brown because he was standing
right there when Delaware told you. The Bel Air. I heard Delaware

tell you, so I know that his killer must have heard him too. And once he found Delaware he could find Lilah."

Scratch was coming out of the house as I explained it. I got off Lacey's back, and he scrambled to stand beside me as we watched him approach. Slowly and deliberately, he strolled down the overgrown path, like a man with killing on his mind.

15

It was his eyes that told me—those evil, sleepy eyes. It came back then.
The Stamp and Go, the way he'd leaned against that bar, and I knew
then who he was and what he had done. I was hypnotized as he came
toward us, the way they say a bird is by a snake before he strikes her
dead. His right hand hit the side of his leg as he walked, strumming it,
knocking out some silent rhythm that made no more sense than the
words he'd written on Lilah's walls. The other hand held his hideous
knife, which he held loose and menacingly, like a street fighter does.
It glimmered as it caught the sunlight.

There was blood on the knife.

All life had been sucked from the air. I could hear only the crunch
of his feet on the grass as he approached. I wondered if my fear had
done that, made everything but the sound of his coming disappear. The
sun beamed down as hot and bright as molten glass. The sweat rolling
into my eyes from my forehead stung. My heart beat fast.

There was nothing in his eyes but death. I thought about what Hannah Grant had said, how he had slammed the German's nose straight

through to his brain, and I knew what Delaware and Lilah had seen in his eyes in their last moments of life. I thought about Raythell Broom and cursed myself for my lack of insight and intuition this second time around, for not seeing him for what he was the moment I laid eyes on him, for not knowing what could save my life. My heart beat so fast I was sure he could hear it.

What kind of man killed like that? Where you can see the life flow out of another. Where you can watch a soul leave a body and feel nothing but satisfaction.

I'd stood beside McDermitt that day we'd met Raythell Broom, knowing the evil that had come into our lives like some foul smell, and I stood beside Lacey now, unlikely allies, both of us aware of what we had in common, that we were as different from Scratch as McDermitt and I had been from Raythell Broom.

Lacey was breathing heavily, as if he'd been running, his breath coming from the bottom of his chest. His nose was still bleeding, and he wiped it nervously on the back of his hand, and then absentmindedly on his pants. His arm brushed mine. I could feel him trembling. He was a skinny man with no spare flesh on his body. He had sized this man up—what he knew of him, what he'd seen that night in the bar, the way men do: *Can I take him? Can he beat me?*

We both knew the answer to that one.

He shifted his weight from one foot to the other, like a small boy does when he has to pee. I was smarter than Lacey, I knew that, and tougher, but because he was a man, if there was a physical challenge it would come from him. I wondered how long it would take before he tossed me to him, told him some lie to exchange my life for his.

"You know what I come for," Scratch said. The British accent was gone, and the words were spoken in the melodic tone of his native country. "You know what I come for." They were words that could mean anything.

Had he come to kill us both? Was he asking us about the money? But didn't he already have it?

Lacey stiffened and threw me a quick sidelong glance.

"Man, you got your money," he said, his voice frightened but reasonable. "Why don't you just leave us be." You could hear the terror, and I would have been embarrassed for him if I hadn't been so scared myself. He watched that knife too, the way it gleamed in the sun, the blood that was caked on it. There was blood on Lacey's vest, too, and bruises on his face. It was fresh blood, still red.

Scratch studied Lacey as if he hadn't heard him or didn't understand what he was saying.

"I don't have shit," he finally said.

He was standing near us now, but he was smart enough not to stand in front of that pool. I backed closer to the bushes behind us. He looked bigger than he had inside, or maybe my fear had added to his height.

"You know what I come for."

"I *don't* know, man! Tell me," Lacey begged. I was silent, wondering about that cut on his face and the blood that gleamed on his vest and on that knife. There were two of us, but his thick body blocked any possible escape. And there was that knife. I thought about taking off down the path that Lacey had come up. If I could make it into the bushes that grew behind the bench, I could make it off the property, but somehow I knew the first one to move would be the first one to die.

I was certain of two things about him: He liked the smell of fear and he liked to kill, like a cat who likes to play with his prey, batting it around to make it run so he can thrill to the joy of the chase before he devours it. Maybe Lacey sensed that about him too, because neither of us risked a move.

I also knew that everyone has a weakness. I had found Lacey's earlier, and if I watched this man long enough, used every instinct I was blessed with, I could find his out as well. Then would be the time to make my move, whatever it was to be.

"I want what I come for." There was no emotion in his voice when he spoke the words, no feeling or change in the way he said them; he spoke them exactly as they had been spoken before.

"What you talking about, man?" Lacey asked, that high voice squeaky and unnatural.

"I come for what is mine."

"You the guy who was next to Heinz in that bar, ain't you? I thought I recognized you, man." Lacey bowed his head in deference, in what could pass for respect. "I thought it was you, man. You probably the man, ain't you? The man that Heinz, you know who I'm talking about, that German dude, was bringing the money to? I know I shouldn't have taken that money, man. I'm sorry, man. I'm sorry. But I don't have it now, if that's what you're looking for. But it should be back with you? She said the money was back with you, where it belongs. If you're still looking for it, though, I just don't have it, man." He made a helpless gesture with his hands. "I just don't have it."

He was pleading for his life with every gesture he made and every word he spoke. He shifted backward, falling against me. His hazel eyes were wide and moved fast, like a junkie's looking for a fix.

I wondered if he was going to turn and push me toward Scratch, using me as a shield so that he could make a run for it, leaving me to face the big man by myself. I wondered where Basil was, if he had come, if I'd actually heard the sound of his bike. But if he had come he would have been down here by now. I would stake my life on that. Unless something had happened to stop him.

My eyes went to the bloodstains on Scratch's shirt.

I couldn't breathe for a moment because I knew suddenly where those stains had come from.

It was Basil's blood. It had to be. It wouldn't be Bettina's if she had come back. I had heard his bike. What had happened in that house when Scratch left the window? Scratch's eyes followed mine to his shirt.

"So you with Bettina, eh?" I knew with those few words what he was telling me, taunting me without saying it.

What had happened in that house?

The thought turned my heart inside out, and it ached suddenly, the pain dull and complete as it filled every part of me. I had felt pain like that before, when Johnny died, when my son's half brother Hakim was murdered.

Had he killed him?

I felt weak, and so powerless I wasn't sure I could stand.

Don't think. Don't think, I repeated to myself.

I fastened my eyes on Scratch's now, defiantly but saying nothing. I knew he wanted to see my fear, and I kept that from him. I stared at him, my mouth in a tight line, focusing all the hatred that was in me toward him. Hatred for everything I knew about him, everything I didn't.

If he had hurt or killed Basil there was nothing I could do now. I had to get away from him. I had to save myself. Some small sane part of my mind whispered that truth to me.

I lifted my head. Meeting my will with his. Getting my strength from somewhere deep within me. If he wanted to kill me, let him. I wouldn't beg him for my life. I remembered something Johnny had told me once about how power respects power. During slavery, he'd said, it was never the strong slave who got beaten but the weak one, the slave who cowered, who feared the lash more than betraying or losing his self-respect—who was defeated before the game even started. I thought about that now, as I faced down Scratch, looking him in the eye without flinching.

"I don't got nothing that belongs to you, now," Lacey cried, his eyes on the knife. Scratch held it in front of him, right under his nose now, a smile playing on his lips. "I had it, man. I had it but it's gone now.

They took it from me, man. If I still had it, I'd give it to you, man. Somebody stole it from me, man. Somebody stole that money from me! I ain't saying I had any more right to it than anybody else. I—"

"Where is it?"

"Her! You got to ask the girl, man. Ask the bitch." Lacey screamed out that one word as he pointed at me; his eyes glanced around from side to side, like he was looking for somebody to back him up in his accusation.

I almost felt sorry for him, even as he continued, pointing at me, squealing at the top of his lungs, sounding like some terrified little girl.

You weak-ass son of a bitch, I thought. *You dirty little chump.*

"Her. She was with them. She knows where it's at. She told me she knew. Let me tell you how it went down, man, all right? I was with my man in the bar, you know who I'm talking about, the German dude, the blond guy. I was a friend of his, you understand. Remember when she came in with Delaware Brown and them others?

"I didn't know it was yours, man. I didn't know that money was yours. Those kids took out those lights, man. Next thing I know, my man drops dead. Right smack dead, right against me, man. I knowed the fool. I couldn't get it straight. He was a friend of mine, man. I knowed he had that bag of cash with him, so I figured I'd take it. I didn't know it was yours, man, or I never would have touched it. I just thought the money belonged to him, man. I didn't know you were the guy he was meeting," he rattled on, contradicting himself, the lies flying out of his mouth along with the spit.

"I know she has it, man. She told me she has it. She told me! I was just about to find out where it was, man, when she jumped me, man. You know how bitches do? Taking advantage of me, you know how bitches do? I was about to get it, man. And you can have it, man. You can have it all! I tried to get it back, but—"

He stopped as if transfixed by something in Scratch's eyes or maybe some sense that told him what I already knew. In Scratch's world weakness was inexcusable, and a rat was nothing but a dead man, even if he ratted on somebody who you wanted taken out. It was a matter of honor. Honor among those who had never known any.

I stepped backward, watching him now as his eyes focused on Lacey, the knife flashing in the sun. But it wasn't the knife that he used.

Lacey's death came quickly, the way it must have come for the German and for Delaware Brown and maybe even Lilah. There was no warning before it struck, nothing except his movement, as graceful and silent as they make it look in the movies. Like a warrior. An assassin who has no sense of life or fear of death. A step forward. A glance. A quick twitch around the eye, and then the sudden rapid slice of a big hand, taking Lacey's life with a brutal jab into his throat. The backward swing of Lacey's head told me his life was gone. There was no change in his eyes. His fear was still there. The death had come too quickly for even that to change. He crumpled near my feet, like a puppet whose string has just been snapped.

I'm not sure where my mind was. Everything had stopped, everything was frozen. There was no sound, not even the shriek of the tree frogs or the birds. No rustle of leaves or grass or flowers. Nothing, except the silence of death.

I felt a numbness that went deep into my bones. I wondered if I could move. Scratch lifted his eyes to meet mine with a look in them I couldn't interpret. Was it shame? Surprise? Pride?

They were serpent's eyes. Heavy-lidded, slanted, and as cold as any eyes I'd ever seen. Colder and more empty even than those of the man he'd just killed. I watched him now, scarcely breathing, wondering when he would attack, knowing instinctively not to move too fast or suddenly. I watched him like you watch a rabid dog or a snake that is poised to strike.

His eyes left mine as he looked down at Lacey's body. He rubbed his hands together, slowly, and then paused and brushed them on his shirt as if they were soiled. He nudged Lacey's head with his foot as if he were moving a piece of log or a dead animal. He had a distant look in his eyes, his mouth was open, his lips sensually parted as he bent down to Lacey's body. It was obscene, the way he touched his face and then the side of his neck with the back of the hand that had killed him. He still held the knife in the other. He glanced toward me with those repellent slits for eyes, and I ran.

I ran for my life. I ran around the pool, dangerously close to its edge, and headed down the path, nearly tripping on damp leaves and moss, but I kept going. *Faster.* I lost a sandal, and kicked the other one off to keep it from impeding me. I ran barefoot then, over twigs, stones, and broken glass. I didn't stop or look back. I choked back a scream of anguish, holding it, shoving it inside to make me push faster. *Faster.* Down the path. Through the garden. I tripped over the step leading to the back door, cutting my knee. I got back up in the same motion, bumping into the closed door.

I prayed that the door was still unlocked. Willed that it be. I fumbled with the knob, screaming out in fear and expectation, and then it opened. I was in. I slammed it behind me, falling against it as it closed, remembering I had to turn the lock, doing it in the same second that I thought of it.

I caught my breath, still panting from the chase. But there hadn't been any. He walked to the house as slow and deliberately as he'd left it. A smile of pleasure on his lips. He was savoring it. The fear. The hunt. The kill.

I looked around the kitchen. Each moment brought him closer, but I knew that I couldn't leave it. There was no hiding. He would find me if I hid; it would simply prolong my fear, break down my ability to fight back as I cowered from him in terror. This kitchen would have to be our battlefield. *His killing ground?*

The glass from the bottle of Red Stripe that he'd broken on the sink caught my attention and I picked it up, wondering if I could use it. A broken bottle is a good weapon, as sharp and deadly as a knife if you use it well, but it had been broken too near the top. A knife would be better. I threw the dishes out of the sink, and they clattered noisily on the floor as I searched for that rusty knife I'd seen before. Finally I found it, and stabbed the wooden table with it twice, to get rid of some of my tension and make sure it would hold. It went in deep, leaving a sharp, narrow indentation.

He came closer.

He picked up a rock, and hurled it at the house, just for the hell of it, in rage, and it shattered the window. I thought about the way he'd broken that bottle in the sink, and how he had written those words on Lilah's walls.

I grabbed a bottle of Red Stripe from the refrigerator, closed my eyes, and slammed it hard against the sink. The neck broke off in my hand, too close to the top as his had done. I tossed the broken bottle on the floor as beer soaked my hands; the smell of it made me feel sick. I grabbed another bottle and tried again, and this one worked; its jagged edge gleamed from the beer that poured out of it.

I turned to the door. If I could get close enough to him to go for his throat, for his balls . . . I thought about the German again. His nose pushed straight back to his brain. I started to shake.

I wasn't strong enough.

He was outside the door now. I glanced at the windows.

I'd have to face him down.

He kicked the door—once, twice, three times. It cracked straight down the middle, like it does on TV in a cartoon, and he came through it like the monster does. Evil like the devil my grandma used to talk about, and I was scared the way a kid is scared. I got ready, holding the dull knife in one hand, the broken bottle in the other.

He looked at me and smiled.

"So you use that against me?" He nodded toward the knife. "What she use to chop potatoes. A bottle of beer? I showed you what I could do to your friend."

Even if I'd wanted to answer him I couldn't.

"You think that will stop me? Nothing will stop me until I get what is mine. I told your boyfriend that."

Was he talking about Basil or Lacey?

I said nothing. He read my eyes.

"You want him? Follow his blood."

I looked straight ahead into his eyes, making mine as dead as his.

Basil must have been here, must still be here. When he came back, he had demanded to know where I was—I was sure of that now. He had fought him. But that was all I knew. I was lost for a moment in a rush of the memory of last night, a biting sadness intermixed with an ache so deep I wasn't sure where it began or ended. I could feel for an instant the touch of Basil's lips, his hands on my breast.

But I wouldn't let myself cry. A wail gathered in the back of my throat. I would have choked on it if I'd tried to speak.

But then a thought came with piercing clarity. *Had he seen the sudden change in my face,* I wondered, *the glimmer that sparked in my eyes? Had I concealed it, that slice of an answer?* I turned to face him, keeping nothing but my fear in my eyes.

"You like a fight, eh?" he taunted me as he moved toward me. "I'll give you a fight if that's what you like, but then it will be over, and you will give me what I want too."

I knew now how I could kill him.

I backed away from him, but I was sure of myself, as sure as I'd been of Lacey outside when I'd figured out how to beat him. But this would be harder, I knew that. I prayed deep in my mind and soul.

Please, please help me, Lord.

He moved toward me, touching me as he came closer, leaning over me, brushing my thighs with his, and I leaned back against the sink, putting up a struggle, brushing up against him but finally letting him grab the bottle and wrestle it from me. I felt the strength in those hands. I hated his closeness. But I let him linger when he touched me, as if I were used to the touch of strange men's bodies.

"I have it," I said, my voice barely above a whisper. "I've always had it."

I was startled for a moment by the sound of my own voice, how calm it was, cooler than I'd thought it could possibly be.

"You play it well," he said.

"I learned it well," I said, not knowing what the hell he was talking about.

"Where else could it have been?"

"You must have known. You're that smart," I said, jabbing to see what I could touch.

He was too close to me. He took the bottle and knife from my hand, and tossed them into the sink. My stomach jumped; his smell, the sweet scent of cheap lemon cologne and beer, made the food I'd eaten earlier rise up to the top of my throat. I swallowed, hard.

"So how you know Basil then, that black bastard?"

"I met him once. Twice. Through Bettina. I'm her friend. I told you that," I said again, looking him straight in the eye as if I had nothing to gain from lying.

"So you with him last night, eh?" The tone of his voice and the sneer in his voice made me feel dirty.

"He means nothing to me."

"I didn't think he was that much of a fool, to risk his life for a woman like you."

I shrugged. "All men are fools."

"You believe that, eh?"

"I know it. Lacey was certainly a fool, wasn't he?" I continued, breaking bad, tossing my head like some outlaw girl in a B-movie, hoping it was convincing. "But when we started together I knew it. He brought the others into it, but I won finally. Like I always do."

I knew enough now about what had probably happened to take bits and pieces and blend them into some semblance of a truth, something that could pass for reality, enough to take him in, to get him where I had to get him. But my heart was beating fast. One false step would be fatal. I wondered what had happened to Basil. If he had actually killed him or just injured him. I wasn't sure how long I could keep up my front.

He stared at me with his empty eyes. I rambled on, making it up as I went, talking tough like some of those young girl gangsters I'd grown up with, taunting him subtly with my body like I'd seen whores do. I had nothing to lose, not a goddamn thing, so I played the game "well," as he'd put it, played it for my life.

"He had it like he said but he never had it for very long. And neither did the girl," I went on, saying one thing that I knew must be true. If this brutal man had confronted Lilah and she'd known he had killed Delaware like she must have known he had, she would have told him anything he wanted to know and then some. Lilah was a greedy little liar, but she wasn't a fool.

But then where was the money?

"The woman?" His eyes looked distant for a moment; I wasn't sure how to read them.

"Which is why she couldn't tell you where it was," I continued, playing what I thought must be true. His eyes shifted, doubt coming into them. His look changed as he stared at me; something in those sleepy eyes told me I'd made some kind of a mistake. I changed directions, back to what I was sure of, to what I knew.

"That's why you didn't find it. Why you couldn't get it from her. I had it all the time."

"Where is it?"

Lilah must have stashed it in her room. Hidden it somewhere he hadn't thought to look.

"Where is it?" he shouted at me again, impatiently, and his eyes changed the way they had before he killed Lacey.

I nodded toward the stairs. "I got it hid. Back in the hotel. Back at the Montego Bay."

"Shit," he cursed under his breath. "Where?"

"You can't get it without me."

"Let's go." He grabbed my arm. "My car is outside. Down the hill."

"I need the key."

"Key?" he asked, as if he'd never heard the word before.

"Yeah. I'm not Lacey. You think I'm dumb enough to leave it where some asshole can find it. I'm not a stupid woman."

He laughed deep in his throat. "I can see that. Get it."

"It's upstairs." He looked puzzled. "I left it upstairs. In the bedroom. Up there." I stumbled over the words, praying that in his greed he didn't notice.

He sensed something. I could see it flash across his face. He had the clear, unwavering instincts of an animal—I knew that much about him. He studied my face, looking for something he couldn't see, and I stared back at him, giving up nothing. He grabbed my arm, roughly snatching me toward him, and I knew he'd done it because he loved the feel of power and how a look of terror could spread across a woman's face. I broke bad, snatching my arm away, tossing my head in defiance.

"What happens to me when you get it?" I asked him. I knew what the answer was but he'd expect me to ask it, and if I didn't he'd know something was up, get suspicious. But there were only two choices. One of us would die.

"What you want to happen?"

"I don't want you doing to me what you did to Delaware and the German. What you did to Lilah."

Again that puzzled look, filled with sudden doubt. I'd played it wrong, but I wasn't sure how.

"Depends," he said. "I like smart women who not afraid of shit."

"You're strong and I like my men strong." As repulsed as I'd ever been by anything in my life, I touched one of his arms, knowing the kind of thing he would expect from "a woman like me," running the tip of my finger along the overgrown ridge of a muscle. He nodded toward the stairs and snatched me, shoving me in front of him to lead the way.

It had started to rain again. I could hear the drops hitting the windows and the trees. A cool breeze blew in suddenly from the open door of the terrace. It smelled fresh and sweet like the spices and flowers that grew on the island. I thought about Jamal and about Annie and Jake and my sister Pet. It wasn't my past that went through my mind like they say it does, but my future—what I'd never see again or feel or think. I closed my eyes tight, blinking back tears, as he nudged me on in front of him, pushing me in the hall before we got to Basil's bedroom. In a sudden moment of practicality, I wondered if my insurance policy was paid up and if I'd ever made it clear to Annie that I wanted her to raise my son. I loved my sister dearly but she and her husband had enough on their hands without Jamal grieving for his crazy mama who had gone and gotten herself killed by some madman while she was on vacation.

"Which one?"

I nodded toward Basil's bedroom, unable to trust my voice.

He shoved me in ahead of him.

"How long you been in the life?" he asked, as if coming into the bedroom had reminded him of my sexual availability.

"Long enough." I moved toward the bed, him following behind me. He pulled me to him. I pulled away instinctively, then realized I'd made a mistake. I'd have to play it any way he wanted it played. They were his rules. He ran his hands over my body, lingering on my breast, stroking my throat. His hands were as cold and hard as you'd expect a killer's to be. Repulsed, I cringed from them, but he didn't seem to notice it. Or maybe it just added to the attraction.

"So you like it?"

"Depends on who I'm doing it with." I pulled away, and he let me go.

"How long you and Bettina been together?" I asked him.

"Long enough. Get the key."

He stood above me, too close for me to breathe.

Brushing his leg, I knelt down by the square, squat night table, made of carved mahogany with its brass handles shaped like flying fish.

He snatched me up to face me suddenly, as if his animal instinct had warned him. "Don't bullshit me, woman. Don't bullshit me."

"Hey baby, don't worry," I cackled, like a devil-may-care streetwalker. "You think I don't want to live?" I had only one try, one moment to get it right.

I knelt in front of the night table, and his eyes fastened on me as he sat down on the far edge of the bed.

Which drawer had it been in? Which had I opened by accident last night? Had it been the bottom or the top? All I needed was to come up with a handful of condoms instead of a gun.

Basil would put his gun in the top drawer, I decided; being able to grab his gun quickly would probably be more important to him than grabbing a rubber. I pulled it open, shifting my body to hide my movements from Scratch, arching my shoulder and stretching my arm as if I was trying to find a key taped to the top of a drawer. Praying.

"Where did you put it?"

Thank you, Jesus! I had it.

"I taped it to the top of the drawer." The gun was solid and heavy as I worked it into the palm of my hand. It was a .22, a double-action revolver. I could tell that by the shape and size of it. A "lady's special," the old guys used to call them. Small, but lethal at close range. But I'd known big men to take two slugs from one and still be able to get up and choke the fool who was holding it.

But it was all I had. I prayed it was loaded.

"You got it?"

"I got it."

He started toward me, and I spun around, fast, moving out of his way, pointing it at him as he grabbed for it. He dove for me, knocking me against the wall, and I pulled away, keeping my gun hand out of his reach, pain shooting through my fingers as my elbow slammed against the nightstand. I twisted around and fired. The shot hit him in the arm, and he glanced up at me, a look of shock and surprise on his face. He touched the blood that was seeping from his arm like he didn't quite get it, and then he glared at me with a fiery rage that told me I'd have to kill him the next time around. I scrambled on all fours to get out of his way, turned around and shot him again. I aimed for his heart, but hit his shoulder. He smiled at me like he knew I was doomed. I took a breath, deep to calm myself, looked straight at him, supporting my right hand with my left to steady it, get the cleanest, surest shot I could, and I fired again—once, twice—and then he dropped.

I waited for a minute or two. He didn't move. I crawled over to where he lay, not sure what to do, what to feel. Killing would never come easily for me, even in self-defense.

I studied him for a while, not saying anything, as his life flowed out of him. Maybe it's because I know that life is precious, and because of what I've seen of living and dying, but I believed I owed him something for taking his life. I owed him the truth and a few last words of comfort, I decided, even a killer like him. I guess that's just the way my grandma raised me. I bent down to him, sure now he couldn't hurt me.

"I'm sorry," I said softly. "But I knew you would kill me like you killed the others. The truth is I never had your money. I never did. I don't know what happened to it. I'm sorry that you had to die for it, though. Do you have anything you want to tell me? Say to me?"

He cocked his head and stared at me, his eyes blinking, his breath coming in pants. He chuckled a low, hoarse chortle that sounded more like a death rattle than anything else. He spoke so low I had to bend close to his mouth to hear him.

"So she had it all the time," he said before he died.

I was too numb to feel anything, even fear or hope, as I followed Basil's blood like Scratch had told me to, not sure what I would find. I found him lying sideways on the terrace off the living room. He had dragged himself outside through the open door. He was bleeding, but he wasn't dead. I sat down beside him, taking his hand in mine. I felt like crying, both in gratitude and grief.

"You shot the bastard?"

I nodded.

"I'm sorry I couldn't get—" He winced in pain, and I held his hand and kissed his smooth, hot forehead. "He surprised me, I tried—"

It's all right," I said. "I'm okay."

"Don't cry for me," he said. "I've been through worse than this. I know what will kill me and what won't, and this won't come close. It's blood, that's all. But you listen to me now. Listen!" His voice was suddenly stronger, and his hand tightened on mine. "Leave now."

"No, I—"

"Listen to me. Get the gun that you shot him with. Bring it to me. It will look like we had a fight. He came in. He killed the other man. He tried to kill me. I managed to shoot him with my gun."

I listened numbly, bending close to his lips so he wouldn't have to strain.

"But I want—"

"No! Give me the gun, Tamara. Listen, your things are in the trunk of his car. Take the bike." He reached into his pocket and shoved the keys to his motorbike into my hand. "Drive it slow, watch for the holes.

Go back to your hotel, and then get out of the country. Your things are in the trunk of his car," he said again. I wondered if he was delirious, what he was talking about, but he continued.

"Listen to me! He parked it down the road. His car. I came back up here, something about what Bettina had said. I knew he might be coming. I didn't want you to be alone with him." He paused and glanced away.

"Never mind, you can tell me—"

"There's no time, listen. I broke into the car—all your stuff is there. Your bag. Your passport. Even some photographs of you and some others. Everything you need to get out of this country. He cut me bad, but he's dead, and I'm not. Go! Take the bike and go."

"But I'm not going to leave you. I can't—" He pulled me to him before I could finish, and his breath touched my ear as he whispered.

"Tamara, if you stay here, waiting with me, they will connect you to the others. Think of your son. He needs you there. Listen! This killing will lead to everything else that has happened. You will be down here for weeks while they sort things out, talking, explaining, paying people off. There will be no loose ends this way.

"When you get down the hill, call the police. There's a gas station two, three miles from here. There is a phone there. Tell them nothing but that there's been a shooting and two men are dead and one is badly wounded.

"It is good Scratch is gone. His brother will be glad to be rid of him, and you have saved my sister's life. I will get in touch with you when this is over. Don't worry about me."

I lay down next to him, warming him, feeling his strong body next to mine. Suddenly, in a swift stab of desire, I wanted him more than I'd ever wanted anyone in my life. We lay close for a moment longer, and he kissed me deeply and tenderly.

"I have no doubt that we will be together again, Tamara Hayle. Don't you know by now that we are each other's destiny?"

I left him then and did what he'd told me to do. I found the empty black duffel bag and my Kenya bag with everything in it in the back of Scratch's car, rode the bike to the gas station, where I called the cops, and then finally to my hotel so I could catch a plane back home to be with my son. Basil was right, of course. But I felt nothing but sorrow.

16

She had it all the time.

They had been the last words spoken by a dying man, so I couldn't forget them. They'd played in a corner of my mind as I rode down the hill. I was still hearing them as I parked Basil's bike near the hotel, and as I sealed his keys in an envelope at the desk and left them for his cousin Mavis. I tossed the words around in my head as I packed and as I stood in line to pay my bill.

Was he referring to me? I wondered. *Did he actually think that I was lying to him, making one last mean attempt to trick him?*

Or had he simply and finally understood what I was sure had happened, that Lilah had found a place to hide the money where he hadn't thought to look. In Delaware's rented car, maybe. I was sure she'd taken the keys and driven it back to the Montego Bay. Maybe she'd hidden the money in the trunk or under the back seat. There was some comfort in believing that some parking attendant down on his luck would be searching the car one dreary day and find "all that loot," which would change his life and luck forever. Maybe something good like that would come of it after all.

Wherever it was now, I didn't care anymore. There were questions that would never be answered about this whole mess, and that would be one of them.

So she had it all the time.

Maybe those words had meant nothing at all.

I called Annie and told her that my Kenya bag had been found and, amazingly, the contents were intact, and that if she hadn't managed to send the money not to worry about it. As close as we are, four hundred dollars lent, even in an emergency, is still four hundred bucks. I could tell by the relief in her voice that with all that was happening in her life she hadn't managed to wire the money yet and was glad she wouldn't have to.

Luck was with me regarding my flight home. I exchanged my ticket for one on a plane that was heading out that night. It stopped over somewhere for a couple of hours, but I made reservations on it anyway. The sooner I got out of the country, the better off I'd be.

I couldn't stop thinking about Basil, but I knew his words were true. I would see him again, probably when I least expected and most needed to. For better or worse, he was right: some part of me would be part of him forever. I knew it in my bones and in my soul.

I had no trouble from the Montego Bay when I checked out, no hint of suspicion or questions. No policemen stopped the cab as I headed to the airport. No detective waved papers or flagged me down or forced me into a hot, narrow room to grill me about the last few days. I was home free. The protective spirit who sits on my shoulder was still parked there.

But I was suffering from some form of posttraumatic stress, and I knew I'd probably be dealing with it for a while. When the cabdriver asked me on the way to the airport how I'd enjoyed my trip to Jamaica, I was struck dumb for a minute or two, the experiences of my last days so fresh and painful I couldn't form thoughts, much less words to describe them.

But I knew I'd have to get it together by the time my plane set down in Newark. So I forced myself to answer him the way a happy tourist would: Yes, I'd be coming back, I had a good time, I'd done this, I'd done that—giving the pat traditional answers that he'd probably heard a hundred times from sunburned, hungover tourists. They were the kind of things I'd have to say to Annie and Jamal when they met me at the airport. A forced smile. A lighthearted phrase or two. But never the truth. Never. I would keep that inside me, as deep as the memory of Basil's last kiss. The real deal was that even if I told somebody about it, nobody would believe me. Annie would swear I'd gotten sunstroke. Jamal would think I'd been slipped some kind of drug. Better to keep it to myself.

The airport routine helped me out some: the banter with the ticket agent as I exchanged my old ticket for a new one, the light, polite conversation with fellow travelers. It was all so normal, and I pretended to be normal too. The last few days, I told myself, had been a nightmare, and if I said that to myself long and often enough I could convince myself that it was so.

I had about two and a half hours before my plane took off. I wasn't about to head back to the city for another stroll, so I wandered into a little kiosk on the side of the terminal that sold cheap gifts for forgetful departing tourists, and picked through the selection, looking for something for Jamal. I hadn't spent a hell of a lot of time thinking about him while I'd been down here, and I was hit with a sudden pang of guilt. Luckily, he wouldn't have to know that I'd gotten his gift on my way out of the country.

I should have known, though, that things couldn't come so quietly and smoothly to an end. That any three days spent like I'd spent these would end up taking a diabolical twist that would keep me faithfully saying my prayers for the next twenty years.

Surprised isn't the word to describe how I felt at what happened next. You're surprised when somebody gives you a birthday card when it isn't your birthday or picks up the bill when it's your turn to pay. Surprised is what you are when you get on the scale and you've gained five pounds when all you've eaten is fruit and soup for a week. Surprised wasn't the word, and if something like that happens in this life again, I'll be leaving it ten years earlier than I'm supposed to.

"You thought I was dead, didn't you?"

I froze, stunned into silence.

"You saw that dress, that right red thing that Sammy Lee used to bitch about, laying in the pile on the floor of that room, and you thought I was dead?" She giggled.

I spun around, the three souvenir T-shirts I held on my arm as I looked through the rack slipping to the floor. My eyes bugged and my mouth fell open as I turned to face her.

She had the same round, pink-tinted sunglasses pushed down on her nose that she'd been wearing when I met her, but she was dressed conservatively in a tan, longish skirt and a white, long-sleeved cotton blouse buttoned nearly to the top. Her short reddish hair was piled under a large straw sunbonnet. If I hadn't heard that giggle, I'm not sure I would have recognized her. I didn't know whether to give her a hug or slap her across her face. So I just stood there with my mouth hanging open and a dumb expression on my face.

"I looked for you, Tamara," she started to explain, glancing around nervously. "I called your room the next morning. I know I shouldn't have left you—"

"Where the hell have you been?" I screamed, still not having it quite together.

"The Cayman Islands, I just got back—"

"The Cayman Islands! The fucking Cayman Islands? What the hell—"

"Well, if you'll just wait a minute, I—"

"No. No!" I screamed. A security guard looked as if he was getting ready to approach us. I smiled and he glanced away. I didn't want *that* on my case. "No," I repeated, more subdued, shaking my head like a crazed woman. "I don't want to hear anything you have to say. Just leave me alone. Get out of my face!" The slap-her-across-the-face impulse had definitely won.

"Five men are dead, Lilah. And one man who I care deeply about is wounded. Two of those men had, quote unquote, intimate relations with you—maybe more for all I know. Lilah, what kind of woman are you! Go! I don't want you anywhere near me. I don't want to hear anything you have to say. I—"

"I don't know what you're talking about," she said. "I don't know what you're talking about—about all those men dying. *I* didn't *kill* anybody. Are you talking about Sammy Lee and Delaware Brown? I didn't have anything to do with them dying. You know that. Who else are you talking about. Listen—"

"Leave me alone. I don't know you, Lilah, I just don't know you!"

I turned to leave.

"I got that money, all that money. I got it, Tamara. I got it! It's mine, and yours if you want some of it.

So she had it all along.

"Please, Tamara. Please. Listen to me. You don't know it but you're like a friend to me. You've been like the only friend I've had in a long time. Please! Please listen to me!" She grabbed my arm, her eyes opening wide in desperation. I tried to shake her off, but she held on tightly. "Please?"

"Please what? Help a sister out?"

"No! Not that. I want to tell you what happened. Explain it."

"Explain?" I asked, still dumbfounded. "Listen, Lilah, I'm out of here. At this point, I don't know what really happened. I don't care. I'm cutting my losses, glad to be out of this mess still breathing. My good sense tells me that you are bad news. *Bad news!* So get out of my face or I *will* call that cop over there. And even though I don't want no cops in my business, I know you are more at risk than me!" I turned to leave.

"You're going where?"

"Where do you think? Out of here! Out of your presence. Out of the airport. Out of the way!"

"You're not going anywhere, Tamara Hayle, because your plane doesn't leave for another two hours. I checked," she explained, like she was sure of it.

"Oh, Jesus, you're not on the same plane as me, are you?"

"No. I'm not going back to the States on your plane. I'm going to do a little more traveling."

"Well, then have a nice trip, Lilah. May our paths *never* cross again. I don't know what happened. I don't want to know how it happened. Goodbye. Good luck." I turned to leave, and she grabbed my arm again.

"I got in from the Cayman Islands yesterday morning, and I've been checking this airport hoping I'd catch you before you left the country. If I hadn't found you, I would have had to hire somebody to find you for me. But here we both are. It's luck, Tamara. Luck!

"Your luck, not mine, Lilah. Your ass has been sitting on some beach somewhere in the Cayman Islands, and mine has been a couple of sneezes away from hell!"

"I don't care what you think, Tamara, just hear me out! What you think I'm going to do? We're standing here in the middle of this airport, in a public place. I'm by myself. What can I do? All you got to do is listen to me. Let me tell you how the whole thing came down. Let me tell you the truth. You must have some questions."

I paused for a moment. She was right about that. But I could live with them.

"It's better than sitting here counting your fingers until the plane comes, right?'

"Probably not as safe."

"More interesting! Please. Just hear me out. I'm been through hell too. But we're both survivors, Tamara. Despite all them fools against us, we made it through. We beat them all, by ourselves. We're the only ones left standing. You may not want to admit it, but we're made of the same stuff." she paused. "Please!"

I glanced at my watch. I did still have a good two hours before my plane took off.

"Come on," she said, taking my hand and leading me toward the steps up to the first-class lounge. I looked at her in amazement.

"I told you I'm going to be doing some traveling. I'm going to do Rio for a while. My plane leaves about two hours after yours. I'm heading out of Kingston too."

"Rio?"

"I loved that movie—you know, that *Black Orpheus*. They showed it during Black History Month when I was in junior high school, always told myself I was going to get to Rio to that hill where the sun came up when that little boy played his guitar. So I'm going to Rio, girl."

"First-class."

She giggled. "Yeah, girl. First-class! Ain't it something how quick you get used to it?"

"I wouldn't know," I said dryly.

"I only flown it twice—to and from the Cayman Islands, and I swear I ain't flying nothing else." A waiter came over to take our orders. Lilah ordered a Bailey's on ice. I had a diet Coke.

"I guess you want to hear how I didn't get killed by whoever it was who was doing the killing?"

"That's a good place to start." I was doubtful but curious as to what she had to tell me.

"Maybe we should start from where I left you, Tamara, looking for that money in Delaware's room? Maybe I should start the night before when—"

"Wherever you start, Lilah, make it fast," I said irritably. "I'm not flying first-class, and I was lucky to be able to exchange the cheap ticket I had for the one that will take me out of here sooner."

"So I guess you got your Kenya bag back, huh?" she said, patting it as if it were alive. "And all your stuff was still in it? Ooh, you go, girl! You're good! You must have got it from that guy who took it from Delaware's room, the one who killed him. That's how he got the key to my room, I'll bet. To write all that shit on my walls. He got my key from your bag where I'd put it. How—"

"Just tell your story, Lilah," I said. "Never mind about mine."

She took a long, noisy gulp of the Bailey's and started it:

"That guy who Delaware met in the bar came by that night, after we left the bar, after he put that knife through Sammy Lee Love's heart. The guy with the pretty eyes like Delaware had? The skinny one?"

"Lacey."

"Yeah, him. How you know his name?"

"I've got a good memory."

"Well, him. Anyway. He came by with this bag. A little duffel bag, a little black duffel, and he brought it to give to Delaware. I was in the bedroom when he came, but they sounded like they were having so much fun and shit, laughing and carrying on, I came out to see what was going on. And you know what was in that bag?"

"No. Let me guess."

"Well. It was money. Cash. And a lot of what they call bearer bonds. A whole stack of them suckers, and for big money too. Real big denominations. Ten thousand dollars each. Anyway. That was what that bag was filled with. That's what those fools had, giggling over that money like boys at Christmas playing with their Mighty Morphin Power Rangers. Lacey said if Delaware would keep it for him overnight, he'd give him a nice piece of it. They laughed about how much he was renting his closet space out for by the minute.

"Lacey didn't want to carry the bag anymore or take it back with him because he said where he was squatting wasn't too tough, and he didn't want nobody to rip him off, so he said he'd leave it with Delaware, and then come back and get it later on the next day. That was dumb. Real dumb. But both of them guys were fools."

"Fools, Lilah? I thought you were in love with Delaware."

"In love? I never said I was in *love* with Delaware Brown. But I sure liked to fuck him. He was nice to me. Not like that brutal son of a bitch Sammy Lee Love. I guess you could say I was in fuck with Delaware Brown."

I rolled my eyes. "Go on."

"But I didn't want what happened to him to happen to him. Sure, he killed Sammy Lee, but that was no great loss to the world." She paused for a minute. "But he killed him so sudden like. Delaware was a spur-of-the-moment kind of guy. Like impulse-driven."

"Impulsive."

"Yeah. That's probably what made him do what he did."

"Do what?"

"They'd put all that money back in that bag, and put it in the closet. Smart, right? Anyway, after Lacey left, Delaware took that money back out and started counting it again. And then he looked up at me with his eyes all big and greedy, and he asked me what I thought he should do, and I said, 'Do about what?' and he said, 'This money would be the answer to all our dreams!' and I said, 'I don't be dreaming about somebody else's money,' and he said, 'It can take us anywhere in this world we want to go!'

"Delaware said we should take that money. Get up early the next morning, like at the crack of dawn, and just pull out way before Lacey came back to get it. I told him that was a real foul thing to do to his friend, but Delaware said the money didn't belong to him nohow, no more than it belonged to us, and we'd leave him some of it anyway. But we'd take most of it with us and put it in a bank in the Cayman Islands."

"That was his idea or yours?"

A hurt look crossed her face. "I wouldn't do a friend like he did his friends, like the way he did Sammy Lee and Lacey," she said. "Delaware said that in case Lacey came back that night for some reason, we should take the money out now, and hide it. He said we'd get some paper and put it under a layer of cash, so it would be the same weight. We'd leave it for Lacey at the desk the next morning, with something telling him we had to go. He wouldn't find out about it till he got back where he could count it. We'd be long gone with the rest of it by then. We'd be out of the country before he could do anything about it.

"He took one of them pillows off the couch, cut a hole in it with a razor blade, and put all the bonds and most of the cash in that. Then he tore up some papers so it looked like dollar bills, and laid it in that bag and then put two layers of cash on top of it. Then he jammed the zipper so it wouldn't go down all the way, so you couldn't see where the cash ended and the paper began, and he put it back in that closet. I called down to the desk for a needle and thread, and that maid, the one who let us in when we went back together, brought it up. That's how she knew I stayed with Delaware. Then I sewed up all that cash into the pillow. And then we went to bed."

She took another sip of her Bailey's, and sighed and shook her head. "But I couldn't sleep good. I kept worrying about my thing with Delaware, you know what I mean. I could understand what he did with Sammy Lee. He kind of did it for me. He was sick of the way he was always bullying me and hitting me around and shit, and it was kind of in my honor. But for him to double cross a friend he'd known all his life like that? For him to do that to a guy he grew up with, to take the man's money like that . . .

"I started to get worried about what would happen to me down the line. I knew he'd probably double-cross me first chance he got. So I lay there, tossing and turning, listening to him snore. And then it happened."

"What happened, Lilah?"

Her eyes suddenly filled with tears, and she closed them tightly to keep the tears in. "You may think I ain't nothing, Tamara Hayle, that I ain't nothin' but a liar, but I've seen two men I was involved with killed close together like that. You may think I'm cold, but I seen some shit," she said, and she hugged herself, trying to keep the sobs inside.

I wasn't moved. "Somebody broke in?"

"I think Delaware must have left that terrace door open or else somebody popped the lock. I heard something, Delaware went out to see, and said it wasn't nothing. But then he said, he was up and he was going to stay up. He said he wasn't tired; he was too excited about that money, and we had to get out early, just in case Lacey came back early. So he went into that bathroom." She paused.

"And then I heard him yell out, and I heard something going crack, crack, crack like somebody was hitting something. I got out of the bed and hid in the closet. I heard somebody walking around, but I knew it wasn't Delaware because he didn't have on no shoes. I hid in that closet, and I heard whoever it was in the front room, moving stuff around, opening and closing closets. Then he left."

"I waited, Tamara, until it was quiet. Then I went out, to the bathroom. Delaware was laying there with his head busted open. I just started crying, Tamara. He looked so bad, I just got up out of bed with the man, Tamara. He didn't deserve to go like that."

She started to cry again, and then took another sip of her drink. "I figured whoever it was must have surprised him. Maybe he was hiding somewhere. I don't know. I put a towel around Delaware's waist 'cause it seemed indecent just to leave him laying there on the floor with his privates all out and exposed and everything, and then I got out of there. Fast."

"That's when you came to get me?"

"Yeah. I was scared to go back to my room, like I told you. So I came to your room. But when I left Delaware's room, I was sure I left the door open. Somebody must have come in and closed it, because it was locked when we came back."

"Lacey," I said.

"But wasn't he the one who killed Delaware? Didn't he have your bag?"

"No. It wasn't Lacey. I thought it was him at first, but it wasn't him."

"Where do you think he's at?"

"He's dead," I said.

"They're both dead? That guy Delaware called Lacey and the one who killed Delaware?"

"Yeah."

"You sure, Tamara? You sure?"

"Yeah, I'm sure."

She looked at me strangely, as if she was wondering if she could trust me, and then snatched her sunhat and sunglasses off and exhaled dramatically. "Oooh, thank you, Jesus. I can finally take this shit off. . . . How did he die?"

"I don't feel like going into it," I said.

She thought for a moment. "Then who broke into my room?"

"So then you took me back to the Bel Air?" I asked, ignoring her and getting her back on track.

"Yeah. I stayed in the living room to look because I knew whoever had been there had probably been looking for that bag, and he'd found it, which was why he left without coming into the bedroom. I got the cash and bonds out the pillow and I made it out the window."

"Leaving me to find Delaware's body and take the fall?"

"I knew if they found you with his body, they wouldn't blame you for killing him because whoever had hit him was a lot stronger than you.

"But whoever took that bag we rigged took your Kenya bag, too. I'd left it on top of the black duffel bag, so I wouldn't forget to drop it off at the desk in the morning when we dropped off the bag for Lacey. I was going to tell them to deliver it to you at your hotel. But he took them both, the black bag and your Kenya bag, and that was how he got in my room back at the Montego Bay."

"In your room?"

"I think he must have gone over there when you and me were at Delaware's. I think he must have gone back to wherever he was going with what he thought was his money, unjammed that zipper, and been so pissed off he went looking for me. My wallet was in there with my license and my picture. My room key was in there too. So he knew where to find me. He hadn't forgotten me because of when I took his picture. He stared at me so hard when Sammy Lee made him spill his drink. When he saw my picture in my wallet, he knew to look for me. Tamara, if you hadn't agreed to come with me to Delaware's, I'd have been back in my room when that lunatic came looking for me. When I got back to Montego Bay with the money, he'd already been through my room, crazy motherfucker. I was so scared. So scared! I knew I had to get out of there fast, so I slipped out that red dress, grabbed a pair of panties, some jeans, and a blouse, got my passport out of the drawer, and got the hell out. I didn't even check out or anything. I just drove Delaware's car to Ocho Rios. I was scared as hell. I knew somebody crazy was mixed up in this shit. Some crazy man who was as mad as hell because I had his money, and was looking for me. The whole thing started because Delaware went looking for his friend in that stupid club. It's just like my daddy used to say before he died. Life ain't nothin' but a crapshoot. That's all it is. Ain't nothing but a crapshoot."

"It didn't bother you that this maniac might think that I was mixed up in this too and come looking for me?"

"I called you the next morning from a hotel in Ocho Rios to warn you, to tell you to get out of that hotel, but you didn't answer your phone. I called the manager of the hotel. I made my voice deep and gruff, made it sound like a man's, and I told him somebody had torn up a room. Room 314. I knew he'd call the cops, and maybe catch who did it. I was trying to look out for you, Tamara. I know you don't believe me, but I was."

"And after you finished looking out for me, then what happened?"

"Then I took the money and flew to the Cayman Islands. Only the money was all mine. I don't got to share it," she added with a curl of a smile.

"Yes, Lilah," I said woodenly. "It's all yours now."

I settled back in my chair, not sure what to think of her or what to believe. I had no doubt that there were twists in her story—an event, scene, or person she'd conveniently forgotten, like she'd left out Lacey's suitcase full of money at her first telling. But did it really matter?

"There was a lot of money in those bonds like I told you, Tamara," she continued. "A lot of money. You know, in the Cayman Islands, when I gave them those bonds and set up my account, they didn't even ask me all that many questions. I just gave them those bonds and set up that account, and I can get money out of it whenever I want to. It's in my name and can't nobody else get into it but me."

"That's good, Lilah," I said.

"And I set up one for you, too, Tamara."

"For me?"

"When it comes to money, honey, I'm *always* a woman of my word. I told you if you went back over Delaware's room with me, I'd pay you thirty thousand dollars, so I did it. I set up an account for you, and a little bit extra for all the trouble you went through on account of me, at the Mainland Bank right there in the Cayman Islands. I set it up in your name, Tamara. Tamara Hayle, with a *y*. And can't nobody get to it but you, unless they have your personal ID and the password. Here." She jotted something down on a cocktail napkin, folded it, and dropped it into my Kenya bag. "Don't lose it, now."

I finished up the last of my diet Coke and firmly refused the offer of another.

"Lilah, how much of what you've told me is the truth?" I asked as I stood up.

"All of it, Tamara. It has to be. I'm the only one left here to tell it." She smiled and looked up at me expectantly. "You think when I get back to Jersey, we can hang out? Maybe do some clubs, Short Hills Mall, pick up some nice guys, do a little drinking, have a good time like girlfriends do?"

"Not in this lifetime, Lilah Love."

Epilogue

At least when it came to money, Lilah Love was a woman of her word. There actually was an account for a Tamara Hayle in a bank in the Cayman Islands that contained a "significant balance" available to the person with the proper ID and password, which was, of course, THE-MONTEGOBAY, the word she'd scribbled across that napkin.

I felt good about that money at first. But then I remembered how many folks had died because of it and what my grandma said about evil's bloom and its fruit. I got a sour feeling in the pit of my stomach whenever I thought about going down to get it, and that told me that as much as I wanted to keep that money, I shouldn't. I decided to just let it lay.

You don't see men die and expect to live your next few weeks unscathed. It changes you in ways you can't imagine, and I guess my leaving that money alone was one of them. Despite my moral stance, I was still depressed. I'd killed a man named Scratch, putting evil in its place, but I was haunted by all that had happened. Everything looked gray for a while. I couldn't seem to feel anything but sad.

And then one bleak day, I received a tropical bouquet. I was puz-

Epilogue

zled at first, and then realized it was the anniversary of that night I'd spent with Basil. Even though there was no name on the card, I knew who it must be from. It was a wild explosion of colors—orchids, hibiscus, birds-of-paradise—that arrived on a day where everywhere I looked was mud and snow. When I smelled it, all the beauty of the island came rushing back, and I remembered that somewhere warm the sun still shone, and flowers were still in bloom.